# I Don't

Cinthia
Always say I Do
to love
Ella

# ELLA FOX

*I Don't*
© Ella Fox 2017
Enamorado (In Love)
Book One
Mateo & Avelina

ISBN-13: 978-1544928838
ISBN-10: 1544928831

Cover Design: Sommer Stein of Perfect Pear Creative Covers
Editing: Ellie McLove of Love N. Books
Proof: Judy Zweifel of Judy's Proofreading Service
Formatting: Champagne Formats
Blurb Assistance: The Blurb Bitch
Spanish Assistance: Yahaira Martinez

# Dedication

This one is for *Rochelle*.
Thank you for being an amazing friend, sounding board
and accountability partner. Mateo and Ava owe their
literary lives to you. I never would have gotten it done
without you.

## Author Note about the Enamorado series

Enamorado is Spanish for "In Love." Each story in this five book series will be about one of the oh-so-sexy Cruz brothers—Mateo, Alejandro, Rafael, Diego and Joaquin! I have fallen head over heels in love with this amazing family, and I can't wait to share all of their stories with you.

Happy Reading!
xo
Ella Fox

# One

*Ava—Present*

THE SCREECH OF THE INTERCOM ON MY DESK pulled my attention away from the data I was entering. The timing of the interruption was impeccable, so I wasn't about to complain. Hours spent slumped over a computer were hell on my spine. I was delighted for an excuse to take a break and look away.

I quickly rolled my neck from side to side to alleviate some of the tension while reminding myself that I'd wanted a nine to five job. The shrill tone sounded a third time before I picked up.

"This is a case of perfect timing," I yawned. "I desperately needed to stretch and look away from my monitor."

"Uh, Ava?"

My left brow arched at the uncertain tone of Ben's voice.

"That's my name, don't wear it out," I answered dryly. "I feel like you already knew that since you're the one who called me. What's up?"

"There's… well, a man is on the phone for you."

I assumed it was my boss, a man who was a perfectionist unlike any I'd ever known. Whenever he called, it was because something was not to his exacting standards. I wondered if I'd inadvertently messed up a column in one of my spreadsheets. I tried so hard, but like every other employee at Keeping Track, I had been on the receiving end of more than one talking-to.

I stifled a groan. "It's Mr. Gretchen isn't it?"

The sound of Ben's elevated breathing filled the silence. "Um, no," he answered, "this is most definitely not Mr. Gretchen."

"Well, since you're acting weird I have to assume it's someone unusual. Is it the President? Bill Gates? Oh, wait. I know. It's Ryan Reynolds. If I've told him once, I've told him a dozen times not to call me at work—"

"Not even close. This man—he says he's your fiancé."

All the blood left my head, and my heart stopped beating for several seconds. When it resumed pumping, I tried assuring myself I was asleep. Yep, that had to be it. I was having a nightmare. With my free hand, I pinched my thigh, only to wince at the twinge of pain. I wasn't dreaming.

I chanted 'no, no, no' in my head as I struggled to take in enough oxygen to be functional. I was nowhere near ready to deal with him. Surely he wouldn't have tracked me down at work. With me gone, he had to be using the opportunity to explore the bachelor life and live it to the fullest. I'd assured myself he'd be busy dealing with his social calendar that thinking of me would be impossible.

I embraced denial like it was my job. There was some

kind of mistake or whoever was on the phone wasn't him. Maybe it was some other man calling for an entirely different Ava. Of course! Yes, that was it. That could happen, right?

"His voice," I whispered. "Does he sound—"

"Spanish?" Ben supplied. "Yeah."

I'd been about to ask if he sounded like a stubborn son-of-a-bitch, but Spanish told me what I needed to know. The phone fell from my hand, clattering loudly as it hit the desk. I fumbled frantically, knocking a container of pens over in the process. My pulse raced as the pens scattered across the desk haphazardly. My fingers seemed to be made of butter, and my dexterity was gone, so picking them up was impossible. I abandoned the pens and grabbed the phone, clumsily hitting myself in the cheek with it as I brought it back to my ear.

"Please tell me this is just a prank," I pleaded.

My voice sounded shaky even to my ears. I was grasping at straws, and I knew it, but right then I was holding out hope some tabloid hack had found me. In my panicked state, it was the preferable option.

"It's not," Ben insisted. "Besides, it's not like I'd know to make this joke seeing as how over the course of the six weeks you've worked here, you never added anyone to the approved caller list. I realize you're an introvert but not putting a fiancé on your list seems a little odd."

My heart thundered as I tried to get my bearings. They were, of course, nowhere to be found. It was always like this when it came to him. My inner compass always pointed me in one direction—straight to Mateo Cruz.

"I'm not," I denied shakily. "Engaged," I clarified.

The six-carat emerald and diamond engagement ring hidden in a pair of jeans on a shelf in my closet said otherwise, but having possession of it wasn't my choice.

No matter how hard I'd tried, the stubborn jerk wouldn't take it back. Even when I'd resorted to outlandish and ridiculous measures, it hadn't made a bit of difference. In a fit of desperation, I'd once hocked it for ten percent of its value. I woke up the following morning to a courier at my door with the ring. Two days later I donated it to a children's charity. That time I got it back within six hours, along with a thank you note from the charity for my generous cash donation.

I suspected even if I tossed it to the bottom of the ocean like elderly Rose in the Titanic movie, it would find its way back to me within twenty-four hours.

"Well, the man on line one disagrees which means he must be nuts. You want me to tell him to get lost?"

I half-considered it for a fraction of a second, even imagined how easy it would be to bury my head in the sand and allow a male receptionist to tell my former fiancé to shove off. Only as I played the rest of the possible outcomes through my head did I admit defeat. Mateo Cruz was an unstoppable force. He wouldn't go away simply because I refused to pick up the phone.

My sigh was one of resignation. "No. I'll deal with it."

I clutched the handset tightly as I disconnected with Ben and did my best to prepare myself for what was coming. I sat stock still with the phone held over my heart as I made an attempt to corral my emotions. After about five seconds of breathing in and out, I accepted reality—it wasn't going to work. With an aggravated sound, I steeled myself as much as possible and pressed the button to take the call.

"This is not a welcome surprise," I snipped. "What do you want, Mateo?"

I hoped my voice didn't betray my panic. I thought I sounded somewhat normal, but Mateo knew me better than anyone. He was so finely tuned to my every action; I suspected he'd known I was anxious before I'd uttered a word.

"You have had your space," he announced. "Now it is time for us to talk. In person."

The sound of his voice hit my veins like a drug, chipping away at my resistance and destroying my determination in a nanosecond. I wondered what was wrong with me that I couldn't seem to erect a wall between my heart and my former fiancé. My right knee jiggled at what seemed like a million miles an hour as my grip on the phone tightened to the point of pain. Under no circumstances could I be face to face with him. If a simple phone call threw me off, a meeting would be catastrophic.

My heart thundered in my chest like I was about to have a go in the Thunderdome. "Absolutely not," I hissed. "I have zero desire to see you, ever. Go away, Mateo. I don't want to speak to you."

My teeth ground together when he chuckled as if I'd said something pleasant or kind.

"Ah, mi amor. This is good," he murmured. "You have no idea how relieved I am to hear your fire returning. It killed me to see you so lost."

The way his voice reawakened my craving for him terrified me. For nine weeks I'd assured myself daily that

I was learning to feel less. Within forty seconds, he'd disabused me of the fantasy. A frisson of alarm raced up my spine. There was no way I could meet up with him face to face. If his voice could still elicit the response it did, I'd be done for in the same room with him. No. I needed to stay on offense. Meeting up could not happen.

"Don't talk as though you have any idea what's going on in my life," I muttered.

"I know plenty, mi tesoro."

My teeth ground together as I swallowed past the lump of emotion in my throat. His term of endearment was like an arrow straight to my chest. He was lying—I wasn't his treasure.

"How about we talk about what I know," I said defensively. "For example, I knew before I even picked up the phone that you'd still be an overbearing know-it-all piece of—"

The telltale sound of the call disconnecting before I could finish my sentence brought me up short. Pulling the phone from my ear, I stared down at the receiver with a mixture of shock, disbelief, and, shamefully, disappointment. He'd hung up on me without warning. I'd expected him to argue, but he'd given up without a fight. That wasn't the Mateo I knew.

I was still trying to reconcile my disappointment a minute or so later when the door to my tiny office flew open and banged against the wall, rattling the framed photo of Barcelona that hung just inside.

"I tried to explain to him that you're unavailable but *he won't listen*," Ben screeched.

"And I told him to mind his damn business," a too

familiar voice growled. "No man tells me I can not see you, Avelina."

My eyes went wide as Ben moved aside and Mateo strolled into my office as though he'd done it a thousand times, his green eyes flashing fire as they locked onto mine. Nothing had changed. With one look, we were the only two people in the universe. A million butterfly wings fluttered inside of my stomach and chest as I licked my lips and tried to get my bearings. Mateo's eyes stayed on me for countless seconds before he jerked his head in Ben's direction, breaking the spell with the reminder that someone else was in the room.

"Tell him to get out," he commanded.

I knew I should tell Mateo to go pound sand, but I was busy trying not to have a damn heart attack. Relieved to have an excuse to look away from him, I turned my attention to Ben.

"You can go," I said. "I'll deal with Mr. Cruz."

Mateo cursed under his breath, muttering in Spanish about putting me over his knee. I felt my cheeks flush pink as I forced myself not to respond.

I was thankful Ben didn't understand Spanish because he'd have been more scandalized than he already was. It was apparent he had no idea what to do since his eyebrows seemed to have permanently relocated to the top of his hairline.

"Are you sure?" he asked as he took two steps backward.

As anxious as I was, I still had to stifle a choked laugh. When it suited him, Mateo had that effect on people.

"I have him under control," I assured Ben.

My words were nothing but bluster. I most definitely did *not* have him under control. I was in no way prepared to deal with Mateo Cruz, and without the benefit of any warning, I was thrown even more off kilter.

Mateo chuckled darkly, a low rumble of sound I felt in my core.

"Tienes todo de mi," he murmured.

He'd said I had all of him. My heart slammed against my chest like it wanted to break out and go to him.

The door closed behind Ben with a soft snick, and I had no doubt he would be running from office to office to tell everyone what was going on. Word would spread like wildfire, and within five minutes all one hundred and forty closet-sized rooms on the floor would be abuzz. Many of my co-workers would be waiting with bated breath for Mateo to leave so they could descend on me to demand details.

I gritted my teeth and glared at him as I crossed my arms. I'd had my job for six weeks and had only just started to settle in. That was all a thing of the past. Although I was fairly certain Ben hadn't recognized Mateo, I had no doubt someone else would. Once that happened, all bets were off. After all, it wasn't every day a gorgeous billionaire bachelor showed up at the office to claim his errant fiancée.

# Two

*Ava—Present*

I'D EXPECTED MATEO TO REMAIN STANDING SINCE there were no visitor chairs- and no room for any, either- in my closet office. Instead, he crossed the few steps from the door to my desk and walked behind it, positioning himself on the edge where he casually reclined with one foot crossed over in front of the other. When he looked down at me, I sensed his eyes were cataloging every inch of me there was to see.

I felt stripped bare and completely open to him. He saw too much, and I damn well knew it. The sensual and delicious scent of his cologne wafted toward me, enticing my senses with its familiarity. I bit the inside of my cheek as I tried and failed to keep it from affecting me. Nothing had changed in the time I hadn't seen him. He was as handsome as ever, even though I did note that he looked drained. I assumed he'd been working too hard and had probably flown all night. His usual permanent five o'clock shadow was on the verge of being a light beard. It made him look rugged and sexy, which annoyed me to no end.

I knew it was dangerous to stare at him for too long because if I didn't keep my guard up, I would get sucked into looking him in the eye and from there, I'd be lost. Clearing my throat, I forced myself to look away from his face. The top two buttons of his dark dress shirt were undone, and the sleeves were rolled up, which led my eyes down to his exposed forearms. The stainless steel band of the Patek Philippe on his left wrist left my mouth desert dry. I'd given him the watch shortly after he asked me to marry him. The inscription on the back of the watch read *As every minute passes I will only love you more.*

My natural instinct was to touch his exposed skin, to feel the heat of him beneath my fingers. Glancing down at his slacks, I swallowed hard when I saw the way the fabric of the midnight blue dress pants showcased his thighs. My own clenched as I pictured, in vivid detail, the rest of what those pants covered. I silently cursed the gods for making him so irresistible to me. I hadn't felt arousal in months, but suddenly my senses were rousing from their long slumber, which made me anxious.

When I looked back up, I felt poleaxed. The expression on his face was tender, like seeing me meant everything to him. I felt the walls I'd spent so much time erecting shake on their foundation.

No. I could not allow myself to be so easily manipulated. Hardening my resolve, I forced myself to be strong. He was a bastard, and anything he presented to the contrary was nothing but a lie. It was all smoke and mirrors, and he still thought I was a fool.

"Why are you here?" I snapped.

His lips quirked up into a half-smile. "You know why I am here, mi bello amor."

It hurt to hear those words coming from his mouth.

My balled up fists clenched so hard that my fingernails dug into my palms. "Don't call me that. And no," I countered, "I most certainly do not know why you're here. Stop playing games and get to the point."

He tsk-tsk'd, his eyes full of fire as he crossed his arms over his chest. "If anyone here is playing games it is not I. You wanted me here, Ava, so here is where I am. That is how this works. I know you remember. You call, and I come, always."

My heart softened at the memory of the first time he'd said those exact words to me. I'd called him at the office and asked him to play hooky with me. Five hours and two movies later, we both had stomachaches from gorging on nachos and popcorn at the theater. Even still, we were both laughing as we made our way to his car.

*"Aren't you glad you left work for all of this?" I teased as he opened the passenger door for me.*

*He pulled me into his arms, his hand sliding down to my lower back as he brought me in close. His eyes were full of emotion as he looked down at me.*

*"Yes, I am glad. I would walk through hell if I believed it would make you smile. This is how it will be with us, forever. When you call, I will come. Always," he'd answered.*

I gritted my teeth and reminded myself that it had all been lies. Knowing I had to focus on that, I pushed away all the good memories and stared at him dispassionately.

"I didn't call you," I said emphatically.

He gave me a wry look. "Yes, you did."

I glared at him before quickly looking away.

"Another lie."

"Did you not go to dinner with a man last night?" he questioned. "Do not pretend you were not acutely aware before you even left your apartment with him that I would be showing up. That man will not touch mi tesoro."

My agitation grew at his assertion that I was his treasure. It would have been so easy to tell him it hadn't been a date. I refused to give him the satisfaction.

"I am not yours. I left! You said you would leave me alone," I reminded him. "Once again, your promises mean noth—"

He leaned forward lightning fast and set two fingers against my lips. "My promises to you are sacred, Ava. I have held up my end of the agreement to the letter until today. You are testing my patience with these outrageous claims."

Good. I hope I tested him right on out of my life. I shook my head, dislodging his fingers as I tried to find my equilibrium. I hated him for not being a big enough man to admit how he really felt. He needed to respect my decision, and walk away.

"You said you'd give me time away but only nine weeks have passed. What kind of space is that?"

He closed his eyes and breathed deeply before answering. "It is the kind of space that never should have happened to begin with. I gave you what you wanted for as long as I was able to endure it. Right up until your security team called and told me you went on a date with some idiot. All bets were off then—as you knew they would be."

My eye twitched as I glared at him. "Security team," I spluttered. "Never once did you say you'd be having me followed!"

His brows went up as he dismissed my anger with a wave of his hand. "If you thought I would let you go without a security team, then you were willfully ignorant. You should have known I would never play fast and loose with your safety, especially not after what happened. You are mine to protect."

I gritted my teeth as I mentally chastised myself. He was correct about that, at least. I'd been incredibly foolish having imagined I was alone.

"That's just ridiculous," I argued. "You're the one who needs security. I'm so far off the grid here I might as well be non-existent."

"There is no way for you to know that for sure," he countered. "Especially not after what happened to you."

I pinned him with a glare, unwilling to discuss that at all. He ignored my expression and pressed on.

"Have you remembered anything else from that day?"

It had been posed as a question, but I could tell he knew I hadn't remembered. Still, I shook my head to confirm that he was correct.

He had nodded his understanding before he spoke again. "Now more than ever, we know the danger our financial situations put us in. Some lunatic could decide to kidnap you at any moment. Security is our way of life, no exceptions. Protecting you is my responsibility, and I do not take it lightly. If something were to happen to you again…"

I looked away, unable to maintain eye contact because

the emotion in his voice caused my stomach to churn. I couldn't think of that day. No matter what my therapist said, I knew remembering wasn't going to resolve anything for me. My gut told me it was best to put it out of my mind and move on. Any time I had a flash of the screech of metal or the shattering of glass, I panicked, often making myself sick in the process.

"I don't want to talk about any of that. I don't want to think about security or accidents or any of this," I said jerkily. "But what I do want to discuss is why you're even in the States right now. It isn't one of your scheduled times to be here."

He cocked his head and raised his eyebrows as he stared at me in disbelief. "Ava," he said huskily, "you are here. Did you honestly imagine I could be so far away?"

"I assumed."

In fact, I'd been positive he would've stayed in Spain. It was where the headquarters for Cruz Saez were located, although there were international offices in New York, Los Angeles, Chicago, London, and Paris. Mateo oversaw the New York branch, but normal protocol found him in town every two months for three or four days, maximum. While that schedule had been built around me, I still couldn't imagine him being away from Barcelona for weeks on end. His announcement that he had been in town the entire time stunned me.

"You assumed wrong. I will *never* leave you, mi amor. Wherever you are is where I have to be."

It was like taking a kick right to the heart.

"I should be allowed to live my life," I said as I turned my head back his way. "If you had any honor, you'd leave

14

me alone!"

I knew I'd hit a nerve by the way his body went rigid. The tension in the air was palpable.

"Soy un hombre de honor."

Calling himself a man of honor! His words sent white-hot rage through my veins.

"Get out," I demanded. "I am over your lies, Mateo. I see through them!"

"You see nothing," he growled, his Spanish accent thick due to his frustration. "But you will. This charade ends today, Avelina. You are coming home with me."

I smacked my hand down on my desk, sending a few of the pens that had spilled earlier tumbling to the floor. "Why are you so damn stubborn?" I demanded. "This is ridiculous! You didn't want to marry me, and you never intended to honor any vows we would've taken. You were doing this for your father and mine, but there's no need to continue. We both know you will survive just fine without our union. I live here now, and I'm not leaving. This is my life—you're not a part of it."

When he straightened, I thought he'd leave. I hated that my first reaction was disappointment. Instead of leaving, he gripped the arm of my desk chair and turned me to face him. He then crouched down and set his hands on either side of me.

"Eres ciega," he murmured.

He'd said I was blind. I shook my head, denouncing his words.

"I told you I wanted you to be my wife long before your father asked us to marry," he stated. "You know this to be true. Deny it all you want, but do so knowing that you are lying to yourself."

My eyes narrowed. "I'm not."

"Tu hogar es conmigo, mi bello amor."

Your home is with me.

With him so close to me, there was a part of me that wanted to believe him. Certainly being at his side was the most at home I'd ever felt. At least it had been until the bottom dropped out. I turned my head so he wouldn't read the emotions in my eyes.

"I can't trust you."

He cursed under his breath as he stepped in closer.

"I am not the one you need to doubt," he answered. "I would walk through fire for you, Avelina. You should trust me above all others, the same way I trust in you. I am not the one responsible for your pain and I would die before I ever caused you harm. Think, mi amor. Remember."

My heartbeat accelerated as a flash of a memory played out in my mind. I shook my head frantically, forcing it to stop. I couldn't think about it. That day was over, and I needed to let it go, forever.

"I don't want to go anywhere with you, Mateo. Stop this craziness. Please."

My voice betrayed me, cracking at the very end.

He reached out and cupped my face with one hand, turning me, so I was looking at him.

"No tienes otra opción," he said firmly.

Being told I had no choice stung like a bitch.

"Why did you let me go if you were never going to give me a chance to make a life?" I demanded.

I'd been so certain that without me around he'd move on at lightning speed. Nine weeks clearly hadn't been enough time for him to work out how to get out of our engagement without angering his father.

He made a sound of annoyance as he dropped his hand and stood straight, all six foot two inches of his frame towering over me.

"Letting you leave went against every instinct I had. You were not doing well, and the harder I fought, the more ground you seemed to lose. I did not know how to stop the downward spiral without giving you what you were begging for. Now more than ever I see letting you go was a mistake. All it did was give you time to buy more into the lies that got us here in the first place. That ends today. Your home is with me, and it always will be."

"What do you want me to do?" I snapped. "Quit my job right this second?"

"There is no need," he said dismissively. "You are fired."

"You can't fire me!"

He raised his eyebrows mockingly. "Can I not?"

The penny dropped as the meaning behind his words hit me.

"You have something to do with this company?"

"I am friendly with the owner. When you chose this job, I bought in."

My mouth fell open as I gaped up at him. I was employed by a data entry company in Jersey City where the staff worked in teeny-tiny offices entering information into spreadsheets for hours on end. It had absolutely nothing to do with Cruz Saez, which made it an odd choice to have invested in.

"You know Mr. Gretchen?"

He shook his head. "No, I know Mr. Gretchen's step-son, Nicholas. We went to Harvard together."

"And out of the blue, you bought shares just because I work here?" I asked, my voice rising as I stared at him incredulously. "Are you insane?"

He shrugged, his indifference clear. "When it comes to you, yes."

Unhappy that he wasn't arguing my assertion, I stood and put my hands on my hips as I glared up at him.

"What on earth would possess you to buy into a company like this?"

"You needed a low-key job where no one knew you. I wanted you to have what you needed, but that did not change my need to protect you at any cost. This location was secure, which made it ideal. You are on the top floor, and the employees get their own space with a closed door. It has kept you away from prying eyes and made it easier for your detail to protect you. That made the expense to invest in the company well worth it."

"Why does what I do matter so much to you?" I demanded hotly.

He waved his hand dismissively. "When you see reality as it is instead of the garbage you were hand fed by someone determined to destroy the strength of what we share, you will know the answer."

I wanted to stomp on his foot and smack him upside the head. Why couldn't he just let me forget?

"You'll never stop lying," I snapped. "I hate you for thinking I'm so goddamn stupid. I know you don't want this, Mateo."

His eyes flared as he stepped closer to me. I took half

a step back, only to come up against my office chair. He had me cornered, and there was no escape.

He set his hand on my hip and pulled me against him, his nostrils flaring as he stared down at me. "Eres una tonta."

I needed to be angry that he'd just called me a fool, but I could barely remember my name. Not when he touched me. The heat in the office rose exponentially the second we made body contact.

I could feel him in every single fiber of my being. My skin broke out in goose bumps, and the hair on the back of my neck stood up on end. I craved him like an addict craved their next hit. As always, my body reacted as though he were the sun, necessary and vital to continued living. My breath hitched as I stared up at him.

"You are wrong, Ava. I want everything you have," he said in a seductive baritone. "Since the moment you turned around in the sunroom, there was never any doubt. It will be that way until I am placed in a pine box for burial. And as I have told you a thousand times, if there is another life after this, I will want you there, too. You are my forever and always. Por siempre y para siempre"

My knees wobbled like freshly made gelatin, so much so that I was fairly certain if he loosened his grip on me, I'd fall over.

"You never really wanted me to be anything other than a warm body," I insisted. "You think I'm an idiot!"

Even to my own ears, my voice sounded breathless and weak.

"No, I think you are perfection," he countered. "You want to know something else?" he asked.

I made a sound in my throat but was unable to form words. It felt like the most natural thing in the world when his hand slid from my hip down to my backside. He had that possessive hold down—as he always had. I shuddered against him as my mouth went dry. When he leaned in close, my brain emptied of everything but him.

"I feel sorry for people who do not have this," he murmured against my cheek. "You are never just a warm body to me, mi amor. You are irreplaceable and without compare. I crave *only you* because I *live* for you. People would kill to feel the way we do. Do not try to deny it."

He was so close the heat of his breath skated across my lips like an invitation to sin. I shook my head, desperately trying to remind myself why I needed to push him away, even though it went against every instinct I had.

"Wh-what are you talking about?" I stuttered.

"This," he answered. "I do not believe anyone else has what we have. I damn well know that no one else knows what it feels like to be so deep inside of you that our hearts beat the same rhythm as everything else in the world fades away."

My traitorous body leaned in closer to his, soaking up his warmth as I blinked up at him like I was hypnotized. My core clenched as I remembered being wrapped around him as he pushed into me for the first time. I'd been a virgin, and there had been pain, but it was quickly overshadowed by the enormity of our union. When Mateo and I were joined, I thought of nothing else but him. It was chaos and comfort all at the same time, in the best way possible.

"Mateo…"

He groaned low in his throat as he pulled me right up against him, leaving no room between us. With his free hand, he cupped my chin. His lips hovered just above my own, our breaths mingling as we breathed each other in.

"Mi amor," he rasped, "I have—"

The ringing of the phone on my desk brought me out of my fog. Smacking my hands against his chest, I pushed out of his arms as though I'd been scalded.

"Stop this!" I snapped.

I smoothed my hands anxiously against the side of my pants, desperate to retreat, but there was nowhere to go. When the back of my legs hit my desk chair I dropped down into it as I tried to catch my breath. Anxious for distance, I picked up the phone.

"Yes?"

"I'm sorry to bother you," Ben said, "but there's a security team here at the front demanding to see Mr. Cruz. Apparently, there's a photographer and two reporters outside."

My shoulders slumped as I let out a defeated breath. So much for getting away. "Go ahead and send them back," I replied.

When I put the phone down, I glared up at Mateo.

"The press is here!" I seethed. "Even for you, this is a low blow."

His brows pinched together as he stared down at me incredulously. "How can you make that my fault?" he asked.

"Don't play stupid! You did this on purpose," I railed. "We both know it. You've taken away my anonymity. There was no reason to come to my work! You already knew you were going to fire me, Mateo. Bringing the press into this is beyond the pale."

"I did no such thing. Nothing was done to bring attention to my arrival—"

Our argument was interrupted when the door to my office opened. I listened as Mateo's head of security conferred with him, explaining that someone in the building had tipped off their brother-in-law that Mateo was in the building. Mateo gave me a pointed look, silently pointing out that he wasn't responsible for the press arriving.

I looked away, unwilling to even acknowledge that I'd been wrong. Another member of his security team produced two file boxes and helped me pack up my desk, something that took me all of five minutes. While I packed, Mateo and the other three members of his team conferred in the doorway.

My fingers twirled the ends of my hair as I stood and waited for them to finish speaking. After sending the team out, Mateo came directly to me.

"We leave together as a unit," he declared.

My teeth ground together as I glared daggers at him. "You can take your unit and shove it right up your—"

"Ah, mi amor, you give me hope. The fire you display is telling me things you do not want me to know."

I looked away and said nothing. Damn him; I knew he was right.

"What do you think Quino would want you to do right now?" he asked.

I went stiff as a board and turned my head back to him incredulously. "Why would you ask me that?"

"Because it is time for you to take your damn blinders

off," he answered. "You and I both know Quino wanted you with me. He believed in us, almost as much as you used to. You will find that faith inside of you again, soon. We are a unit, Avelina. Always. You do not answer any of their questions. Our business is just that—ours. We belong only to each other. No one else."

That wasn't true, though. We weren't a partnership and he damn sure didn't belong to me. I should've come to terms with it, but I hadn't. I knew this because when he spoke, it felt like my heart shattered into a million pieces. I didn't move a muscle as I tried to breathe through the pain.

"You've backed me into a corner," I said pithily. "I have no choice but to come with you for now, but don't expect me to stay."

Mateo said nothing as he took my hand into his and began walking us down the hall. My co-workers were all peeking their heads out of their offices as we walked past, many of them blatantly holding their cell phones up to capture photo or video. I kept my chin up, not looking directly at anyone. I knew they would be talking about me for months to come. It bothered me less than I would have expected. This was partially due to my being in a state of shock, but the bottom line was that when Mateo was around, I ceased to care about almost anything else. That had not changed in the weeks I'd been away from him.

Even though I'd known it was coming, I was not at all prepared for the few photographers and reporters assembled outside. At the curb, there were three black Suburbans. One of Mateo's guards opened the door to the second vehicle as soon as we exited the building, while two other guards ushered us forward. As we walked, questions were called out to us, something I was still trying to get used to.

The press had left Mateo alone until the year before when he'd turned twenty-seven and gained full control of the thirty billion dollar inheritance his mother had left behind. It didn't help that his father was one of the wealthiest men in the world, or that Mateo's backstory was interesting to nosy people. His inheritance made him one of the richest men in the world, his parental situation was intriguing, and his looks made him appealing, which doomed him to being targeted by the press whenever they thought he was doing something worth knowing about. He stayed off the radar as much as possible, but I could see our postponed wedding had peaked their interest.

"Why are you in Jersey City?"

"Ava! Ava! Why did you leave Spain? Have you been here the whole time?"

"How are you feeling?"

"Is there another woman? Did he cheat?"

"Mateo! A source says you were at Club de Sex last night! Can you confirm this?"

Mateo huffed, waving them all off without a word. I turned to glare at him as he slid into the backseat next to me. The thought of him with someone else made me irrationally angry. I was one hot second away from telling the driver to take me to Club de Sex so I could smack the hell out of whomever he'd touched.

"I was not at a sex club last night or any night," he assured me. "I neither need nor want that life, Avelina. All I

24

have ever wanted—all I will *ever* want—is you."

I did my best to pretend like I didn't care even though it was quite obvious I did. I chose to ignore it, instead focusing on something that scraped at my nerves.

"You were saying something about not bringing attention to your arrival," I snapped.

He inclined his head, his eyes predatory as he took his seat and turned to me. "Sí."

"You don't think showing up here with a full security team seemed a little odd? It probably took forty-five seconds for someone to spot you."

He shrugged. "Since your accident, this is the protocol now. I am who I am, Ava. I accept you as you are, I expect you to do the same for me."

I crossed my arms over my chest defensively and looked away. "I accepted you right up until the moment I found out I was nothing but a joke to you."

He came in close, doing away with the distance between us as though it were nothing. His fingers touched my jaw as he gently nudged me to turn his way. I did so grudgingly, facing him with a look of annoyance.

"These lies can no longer hold any power over us, Ava. I will not allow it."

He turned away before I could respond. I watched out of the corner of my eye as he pulled his cell phone out, his screen lighting up as he began scrolling and then typing with his thumbs. The loss of his attention should've been welcome, but I wasn't happy with it. I felt marginalized like I wasn't even in the car anymore.

I wondered why it bothered me the way it did.

# Three

As we got into Manhattan, my suspicion of where he was taking me was confirmed. Sure enough, five minutes later we pulled into the underground parking area for the high rise his penthouse was in.

"We couldn't have gone anywhere else to talk?"

He ignored me for a second or two, his attention still on the cell phone in his hand. I felt as though he was purposely avoiding me, and I didn't like it. When he lifted his head, he shrugged.

"We are not merely talking," he answered. "We are home."

My left hand clenched at my side as I stewed over his choice of words. It most certainly was not my home. It was his and his alone. I'd believed otherwise at one time, but I'd been well and truly disabused of that idiotic fantasy.

I had to swallow past the lump in my throat twice in order to speak. "I don't want to be here," I gritted.

"And yet here is where you are because *here* is where you belong."

I shook my head emphatically. "I don't belong here."

He shrugged. "I am here and you go with me, so…"

I wanted to strangle him for being such a stubborn jerk.

"I'm not a *thing* for you to own," I snapped.

One dark brow raised and his lip quirked as he considered me.

"You are not a piece of property, but I damn well know you are mine," he said. "You yourself have told me hundreds of times that you belong to me, just as I have told you that I am yours. That is my honor, Avelina. Claim me whenever you want, however you want."

Before I could respond or argue—and of course I would have—the car came to a halt. Seconds later the rear door was opened by a member of the security team. When Mateo reached for my hand to help me out of the car, I made an inelegant noise of disgust and ignored him completely.

"I'm not staying here and you should have known I wouldn't want to," I huffed.

He stepped closer and leaned his head into the car. "I know what you wish you felt. I also know that no matter how hard you try, you will never truly be able to walk away. You are not alone, mi bello amor. I would not be able to walk away from you, either. We belong together."

He tried to take my hand again, but I shoved him off. I knew I was playing with fire, but I didn't care. At some point, he would call me on it, but I refused to behave as though I wanted to be with him. I was a fool for feeling that way to begin with. I hoped someday—sooner rather than later, I prayed—I wouldn't care anymore.

After keying in the code, the security team left us at the entrance to the private elevator that went directly to Mateo's penthouse. Since leaving my office, security had been near us the entire time. I hadn't really been appreciative of the buffer they'd offered until it was gone and we were alone. Goose bumps spread across my skin and my breath caught as his unique scent wove its way through my senses. He was too close, too damn male. His larger-than-life presence dominated the space and I had to fight my natural inclination to lean into him. When we came to a stop, I exhaled a sound of relief and all but jumped out of the elevator.

The relieved feeling lasted about two seconds. It faded away as I gazed around and realized the décor was completely different than the last time I'd seen it. Several months before, Mateo and I had spent six straight weeks in New York. During that time, he instructed me to re-decorate the penthouse. I'd never said a word to him, yet somehow he'd known I found the original décor stuffy and rather uninviting. I'd assured him I didn't need to change a thing to be happy, but he'd refused to back down. I'd thrown myself into the project, spending countless hours choosing furniture, fabrics, housewares and accent pieces while working with a design assistant to get it just so. Work had been set to start a few months later; right around the time I left Mateo.

When I made the choice to go, I'd been certain he would scrap all of my plans without hesitation. Obviously I'd been wrong to assume. Before me was the end result of all the hours of work I'd put in designing the space. It was as beautiful as I'd always known it would be. The earth tones and blue hues played off each other perfectly, the penthouse no longer an ode to the colors white and beige. Now it was warm and inviting, a place where you'd want to spend time.

It looked freshly done, not a pillow out of place. I absently wondered if he'd ever even sat on any of the furniture because it sure didn't look like it. My heart slammed frantically against my chest as I stepped forward and looked over a display of photos on the entry table. I'd chosen every frame and every picture, long before the bottom dropped out of my world. I swallowed past a lump in my throat as my eyes ran over the photos of Mateo and I together—some alone, some with our families.

Above the table was a poster-sized photo of the two of us that had been taken at our engagement shoot. In it, we were face to face, his hand cupping my cheek as we stared at each other. My left hand was on his arm, the enormous ring he'd given me on full display. I'd loved the photo from the moment I'd seen the proof. There was no missing the way we felt about each other. It was right there and so obvious how completely in love we were, eyes only for each other.

Seeing the photo shredded my emotions with razor sharp precision and it made me angry. Why couldn't he just let me go? Realizing I was getting worked up, I forced myself to calm down before I blew up. I needed my wits about me.

Through it all Mateo said nothing, but I knew he was taking in my reaction.

"Do you like it?" he asked. "I made sure it was finished exactly to your specifications."

He sounded hopeful, like it worried him I'd hate it. I quickly wrote that off as wishful thinking and forced myself to keep a poker face. I shrugged as though I weren't impressed at all.

"It's fine," I said unenthusiastically as I stepped further into the apartment. "Which prison cell... I mean guest room am I taking?"

When I heard his sharp inhale from behind me I knew I'd struck a nerve. I mentally patted myself on the back for getting a shot in.

"You will sleep in our bedroom, where you belong," he answered.

My pulse raced as my hands shook from panic. I spun to glare at him.

"I'm not sleeping with you!"

He sighed and rubbed at his temples. "Then I will sleep in a guest room for now," he grumbled. "You can have some time to readjust before you admit what it is that you want."

His certainty chapped my ass. "I already know what I want and it's to go home," I said emphatically. "I want *my* space."

It was obvious Mateo wasn't happy by the way his jaw clenched. "No more space," he said thickly. "No matter how many ways you say it, nothing will change the facts. *This* is your home."

"I've got a rental agreement for an apartment in Jersey that says otherwise."

He shrugged dismissively. "That lease was broken and

the apartment is now empty. Your things are in the bedroom where they belong."

"So you just made the decision for me? I don't get a say?"

"I made *this* decision. You made one of your own when you enthusiastically accepted my proposal. Once you remember all you have forgotten, you will thank me for fighting as hard as I have for us."

"I never asked you to fight! In fact, I asked you to leave me alone."

His jaw ticked as he stared at me. "I will not change my mind, no matter the size of the tantrum you throw. You are committed to me as I am to you, whether you want to admit it or not. We are together. Forever."

"We are not together!" I hollered.

I could tell he'd reached the end of his patience. It was in his body language and the expression on his face. I expected him to explode in anger, but he remained composed.

"Tomorrow morning I will set up the earliest appointment available for you to have your wedding gown re-fitted."

Just like that, he took all the wind out of my sails. I felt lightheaded even thinking about putting that dress back on. I'd chosen it in love, had looked forward to our wedding day with such joy and anticipation. I'd been a fool to believe in happily ever after.

"I'm supposed to go all the way back to Barcelona for a dress fitting?"

"It is here," he replied, "at a bridal shop seven blocks down. They will handle this first fitting and then return it to the designer back home."

"I'm *not* marrying you," I snapped desperately. "There's no reason to continue this charade."

He went still as he looked me over like a lion preparing to take down its prey. I knew I'd pushed him too far just by his body language.

"The charade is not mine and I am through being held hostage by it. I have given you time and instead of using it wisely you chose to continue believing lies. The wedding is in six weeks," he asserted firmly. "If you know what is good for you, then you will run down that aisle to me, Ava."

"You can't make me—"

"I can *and I will*," he growled.

"No, you can't."

Several seconds passed before he answered me.

"Thousands of jobs are on the line if you choose to back out."

I wanted to scream. He'd not brought it up before so I'd been certain it wasn't truly an issue. Obviously he'd decided to make it one.

"It doesn't need to come to that. You don't want to be chained to me any more than I want to tie my life to yours. Use your head and—"

"I am done arguing," he interrupted. "We marry in six weeks time. We belong together and that is that. Right now you need to settle in and I need to walk away before I say something I would regret. My intention is never to hurt you."

Without another word he walked away, presumably toward his home office, leaving me behind to wonder when he'd gotten so tough.

# Four

*Four years ago*

I RACED FROM THE JET THE SECOND THE STAIRS WERE down, straight into my father's waiting arms.

"Papá!"

"Mi ángel," he laughed as he hugged me tightly, dropping happy kisses onto my cheeks. "I missed you so!"

I giggled as his mustache tickled my cheek. "I missed you too, Papá! I am so happy we have the whole summer together."

"I am delighted you are home," he said as he set me down on the ground and wrapped his arm around my shoulders. "This summer will be perfect. Anything you want is yours."

All I wanted was to spend as much time with my father as possible. I hated living apart from him, but it wasn't like I had a choice and neither did he. My mother was in charge, and she did not care for Spain even a little bit. Therefore, I lived in New York City with her most of the year. My parents had only dated for a short period—so brief that I had never seen them as a couple. My father had been a forty-year-old widower when he met my mom, his wife Valeria having passed away after having a stroke during a surgical procedure a little over two years before I was born.

As I grew older and got more of the story, I deduced that my father had been in mourning and on the rebound when he hooked up with my twenty-six-year-old mother. They met at some club she was working at and one thing led to another, quickly. I'd once overheard my mother's friend Renee referring to me as a "gotcha" baby. It didn't take much to figure out that meant my mother had set her sights on my father and had gotten pregnant on purpose.

After she announced her pregnancy my father tried to make it work with her, but that quickly blew up. This was not surprising since my mother was the very definition of high maintenance. She'd expected him to marry her but he wasn't that stupid. She was still punishing him for that.

Just three months after my birth they broke up and my mother left the country, and me, behind to return to New York City. She told me later that she didn't enjoy the baby stage and the two years she spent in Spain had been more than enough. I often wondered why she'd ever settled in there to begin with when she hated it so much. My mother was New York through and through, born and bred. She loved the city with a fierce devotion nothing and no one could compete with—including me.

In the years after she had left she would swoop in to visit me for one weekend a month, which had actually been an arrangement that worked. In small doses, I'd enjoyed spending time with her. Then, out of the blue, she demanded custody when I was five.

The transition to her being the full-time parent had been horrible, the stuff nightmares are made of. I just wanted to be with my father but the court had ruled in her favor. My father fought hard and in the end wound up having to settle for getting me for all holidays and school breaks, the entirety of each summer and one week a month when he would come to New York. During that week I would stay in his penthouse, seventeen floors above the five thousand square foot apartment I shared with my mother. As much as I loved having my father for one week a month, I hated that I couldn't live in Spain with him.

Papá pushed for as much time with me as he could get. Quite often the one-week a month he was entitled to would blend into ten days or more, sometimes as much as a month, depending on what my mother had going on in her social life. My father never hesitated to take that time, always willing to rearrange his schedule at the drop of a hat to accommodate my mother's penchant for travel. I did not need to question his commitment to me, or his love, since both were clearly discernable in every one of his actions.

With his arm still around my shoulders, he guided me toward the limo which was parked a short walk across the tarmac. I smiled when I saw the security team waiting for us. I chatted with them excitedly, laughing as they insisted I'd grown prettier in the weeks since they'd last seen me. I didn't believe it for a second—my mother constantly told me that my skin was wretched. I didn't see it quite that way, but I did think the small zits I would get on my chin from time to time were annoying. She was also on a kick about my needing to diet, which was yet another reason I was glad to be out of New York. If I saw one more salad on the dinner table, I was going to scream.

As we climbed into the car, Papá told me his business partner and lifelong best friend, Antonio, had finally finished the renovations on the house he owned next door to our villa. This meant the family had moved back in the previous weekend. It had been a year since the Cruz family had lived next to us, which felt like an eternity to me. Before they moved into their temporary house a few miles away we would all tromp back and forth between our villas, in and out without a care in the world. But then a section of the roof started to leak in the Cruz villa and Antonio decided it was a sign from above to renovate everything. We saw each other a ton after that, of course, but it wasn't the same. Antonio and his wife Camila were family to me. I called them Tío Antonio and Tía Camila, and in many ways I was closer to Camila than I was to my own mother.

There were five Cruz sons. The oldest, Mateo, had only been on the scene for ten years, even though he had just turned twenty-four. He was the son of Antonio's former girlfriend, Mariel. Coincidentally, Mariel's last name was also Cruz, something my father told me she and Antonio had once joked about as far as how easy things would be if they got married. Clearly, that didn't happen. There wasn't a big drama—they broke up because they found they weren't compatible for the long term and that was that.

Mariel found out she was pregnant after they broke up and for whatever reason, had chosen to raise Mateo herself in Valencia, where she had been raised. Financially it wasn't like she'd needed Antonio's input—she had been a shipping heiress with a fortune that nearly rivaled Antonio's. Still, you'd have thought she would have wanted her son to know his father. It wasn't as though there had been bad blood between them or anything—things just hadn't worked out.

Antonio was stunned when an attorney got in touch with him after Mariel was killed in a freak skiing accident. She'd kept Mateo to herself his entire life, but Antonio's name was on his birth certificate and there were instructions in her will about how to contact him if she passed. It had been incredibly awkward at first—Mateo had only been fourteen at the time and he'd grown up believing his mother had been artificially inseminated.

He'd taken to my father long before he'd thawed toward Antonio. Even now, my father and Mateo spoke several times a week and emailed back and forth just as often. I teased Papá sometimes that he should try to adopt Mateo so he'd be able to say he had a son. He would always laugh me off.

"I have you, Avelina. One perfect child was a gift from God. I need no other."

With my father's help, over time Mateo found a place within his family. Papá said most of Mateo's struggles stemmed from being blindsided by so many things changing at once. Losing his mother, finding out she'd lied about his father, then being introduced to his large family. He'd grown up believing he had no relatives aside from his mother. I knew much of that was still an issue for Antonio. He was angry to have lost so many years with his son but there was no way for him to voice that because Mateo wouldn't hear a word against her.

The transition had been interesting all the way around since the family was so large. Two years after Antonio and Mariel broke up, he married Camila. They'd gone on to have Alejandro who was just three and a half years younger than Mateo. Then they'd had Diego and Rafael, who were twins, and finally, the baby of the family, Joaquin, who was named after my father. The Cruz brothers had taken to Mateo like he'd always been there, particularly Alejandro. They spent a lot of time together and I sometimes thought Alejandro seemed relieved not to be the firstborn anymore. Less pressure, he would joke.

I had always been closest to the youngest Cruz boys. Diego and Rafael had been born just five months after me, which meant we'd always done everything together. I spent the majority of my time with them and I always had. Joaquin was sixteen, which meant he could hang out with us every day if he wanted to, but he was always busy playing fútbol. His dream was to play for Real Madrid. As good as he was, I believed it would happen.

Alejandro wasn't around much anymore. Like Mateo, he was away at an American university, so it wasn't like coming home for dinner was easy. Mateo had just finished his MBA at Harvard while Alejandro's sophomore year at Stanford had just ended.

For a long time, I'd harbored a silly crush on Alejandro. Nothing serious, more a case of hero-worship. Alejandro was hilarious and at the time when my mother was at the height of her craziness and my world was caving in, he had gone out of his way to make me laugh. That counted for a lot, and it was why I'd been enamored of him. I was happy that my little crush had finally waned. With Alejandro at school, I hadn't seen him for more than a few days at a time in forever. Even when he was in Spain at the same time I was, he tended to be out with his friends, which was fine with me.

Aside from our age difference, I'd always known Alejandro would never look at me because of how closely aligned our families were. Papá and Antonio owned Cruz Saez, the biggest grocery chain in the world. They'd started in Spain but had begun opening stores in America, London and Paris six years before I was born. Their partnership was about more than business—it was family. Each year for as long as I could remember Forbes would put them on the list of the top ten wealthiest men in the world. Because of this, there were always concerns about security for themselves and their children. I took it all in stride because it was all I knew. Having been born into it, I didn't see how extreme my life was.

Most of that was due to my Papá. I wanted for nothing, but fully understood how lucky I was. He gave tens of millions of dollars to charity each year, but he also put his money where his mouth was and made it personal. Every Thanksgiving since I was eight my father and I had served meals together—all donated by him—at a New York City mission. At Christmas we bought gifts for under privileged children at the same mission, as well as a chain of shelters in Barcelona. Each month we spent one Saturday volunteering our time somewhere. When we were in Barcelona, we would do this with the Cruz family. Papá and Antonio shared the same philosophy, so they had taught all of us to give back, always.

My mother did not share his belief system. Money, she insisted, was something only fools parted with. As a child, I'd overheard my mother telling her friends she would be riding a train of gravy until I was an adult, which was why she would never give me up. Back then I didn't know exactly what a gravy train was, but I knew enough to be sure it had something to do with my father's money.

He didn't realize it, but I knew for a fact he'd offered her money to allow him to keep primary custody. She'd declined. As important as money was to her, I think having continued control over him—as a way to punish him for not marrying her—was her priority.

My face lit up as we took the turn toward our villa. My last visit had been two months before over spring break. Just seeing it at the end of the long driveway settled me. Although I had lived with my mother in New York City for twelve years, my father's house in Spain would always be my home.

"The villa missed you almost as much as I did."

I laughed as I fidgeted in my seat, anxious to get into the house. I couldn't wait to open the door and take in the sights and smells of home. Nothing felt better than being surrounded by the colorful and vibrant things I loved so much.

"A house can't miss a person, Papá!" I teased.

"This one does," he answered.

Being home was the best. I hurried from room to

room, saying hello to the staff I saw along the way. Once I'd greeted everyone, I ran upstairs to my bedroom and threw open the door, letting out a sigh of pure glee as I saw it was just how I'd left it. In New York, my mother had a lavender bedroom for me, and I hated it. In my opinion, it was a color for a young girl and I was on the cusp of being an adult. No matter how many times I reminded her I wasn't a baby anymore, she didn't care. Lavender, she decreed, was the *only* acceptable color for young ladies to decorate with. I disagreed.

At the villa, my room had been redecorated the year before with emerald green accents. It was my favorite color, and I loved the way I'd been able to incorporate it into my room. The richly colored wall behind my bed had been painted using a suede-like textured paint that had some golden shimmer to it. I'd spent many hours lying on my back with my feet up on the wrought iron headboard while I stared at all of the photos of Barcelona I had on the wall.

I kicked off my shoes and dashed for my bed excitedly, throwing myself on top of my green and white comforter with a squeal of glee. The villa was just different from other places in the best way. It was beauty and comfort, a warm blanket on a cold day. I always felt welcomed and loved.

Since I had a complete wardrobe at the villa, I had only one bag to unpack. It was full of books, magazines, a few bottles of nail polish and my laptop. My favorite thing about coming home to my father's was that I never had to bring a ton of stuff. My home received me back in the way that only it could as I settled in happily.

I'd been home in Spain for several weeks and every day was an adventure. Dio and Rafe each had small motor-cycles, so we were able to spend some of our time hang-ing out in the Barcelona city center area. We were nev-er allowed to be out unsupervised, which meant always, somewhere, the security team lurked.

I found it a bit over-the-top, considering I'd been fit-ted with a GPS anklet five years prior and each of the boys had one of their own embedded in their watches. That meant our families and the security teams always knew where we were. I thought that would have allowed us a bit more freedom, but our parents wouldn't back down. I was just relieved the security detail was discreet enough that most people didn't notice them at all.

When we weren't driving around town with me perched on the back of one of their motorcycles, we spent a lot of time going back and forth between houses to lounge in our pools. The Cruz pool had a grotto and a slide, while mine had a diving board and seventy-inch flat screens on either end that slid up from the ground.

Sometimes we'd mix it up by going to the beach. It was, in my opinion, the type of summer dreams were made of. The boys had a group of friends that were al-ways around, which was ideal. Rafael had a girlfriend, Francesca, who lived a few towns over. Her family made her work in their restaurant, so she didn't have as much free time as Dio, Rafe, and I did.

Secretly I was glad of this because she was very

standoffish with me. She made 'jokes' claiming Rafe and I secretly had something going on, when nothing could be further from the truth. I did not look at Dio and Rafe in that way. They were like brothers to me. She had been told this time and again, but she was oddly fixated on me and what I was up to pretty much all the time. Dio called her loca and I didn't disagree. We weren't sure why Rafe was with her because with her penchant for drama and bitchy behavior, she wasn't a blast to be around.

Watching Rafe with Francesca, I realized that my mother was right about some things. Men really could be prisoners to their sexual urges.

Mateo was coming home on Saturday and Alejandro would arrive on Tuesday. Both were staying for two weeks. It was understood that once the boys were home, they wouldn't appreciate a house full of teens each day, so this was a way to let Rafe and Dio have their fun before they came back. The choice to have a nighttime pool party was easy. It would be easy and fun and about thirty people would be attending.

Camila and I spent the afternoon making tapas while the boys set up lawn chairs and put all the water and soda out. I left about ninety minutes before everyone was due to arrive, quickly running home to get ready.

One of my favorite things about my enormous bedroom suite was my bathroom. The colorful Spanish tiles were beautiful and my shower and tub were both large and inviting. Setting my iPod on its dock, I climbed into the shower as Rihanna crooned about loving the way

Eminem lied. I spent a few minutes luxuriating in the feel of the warm water sluicing over my skin. Next, I applied myself to washing my hair and body, the shower taking on the scent of my mango and coconut bath products. I had become addicted to the smell after finding a shop in Barcelona selling non-toxic bath stuff.

After the shower, I set to drying and styling my long hair into a high ponytail. My hair was on the lighter side of brown and my skin would turn pale if I wasn't in the sun, something I'd always found annoying because most people didn't believe I was Spanish. My father's black hair and dark eyed genes had been offset by the gene pool of my blonde-haired blue-eyed mother. From him, I'd gotten my brown hair and my dark eyes, from her, fairer skin and what my father called a button nose. I often wished I'd gotten things the other way around, but with my hours spent in the sun meant my skin was the perfect golden brown.

I sighed happily as I rubbed in my mango and coconut body butter all over my body. There was a little shimmer to it, which made my skin seem like it had a little glow. Being in the sun also meant I didn't need to load up on makeup. I applied eyeliner, mascara and some candy apple flavored red lip gloss and left it at that. In my closet, I chose the dress I'd bought the previous week in the Barcelona city center. It was a patterned navy and white halter-styled maxi dress that I paired with my favorite jeweled Steve Madden sandals.

When I got downstairs Papá was waiting for me in the entryway. He looked tired, as he had for the last week or so, and I said as much. He laughed me off, telling me that the heat of the summer and a hectic time at work were catching up with him. He promised he'd sleep in the following day.

Sliding my arm through his, we chatted as we made our way over to the Cruz's. As usual our conversations were a mix of Spanish and English since we each spoke both languages fluently.

"I love seeing you so happy, mi ángel. Your smile comes quicker when you're here."

"It is easy to smile when I love being here as much as I do, Papá," I answered.

"This is your final year of school," he reminded me. "It is not too late to enroll you with Diego and Rafe here in Spain. If it is what you want, we can make it happen. You are old enough now to have your voice heard, no matter what she throws at us."

It was absolutely what I wanted. I'd long dreamed of going to The American School of Barcelona that the boys went to, but I felt trapped and powerless in my own life. At the end of the day, I felt beholden to my mother. Every time I'd brought up moving to Spain, she lost her marbles. Days of tears and temper tantrums would ensue while she spun tales of woe and being alone. She'd promise to change and spend more time with me. Inevitably I would cave and agree to stay, because I hated conflict and because she was my mother.

As tough as I tried to be, I did love her and I wanted us to have a relationship. Over and over again I'd foolishly allow myself to hope things would be different, only to be disappointed. Despite all of her promises, nothing had ever changed. It was the way of my world.

45

I leaned my head against his shoulder as we continued walking. "You know how she is," I sighed.

"Avelina," he said as he stopped walking, "Karen cannot dictate your entire life. I have never wanted you to feel as if sides must be chosen, so it makes me sad and angry that she doesn't do the same. You are at an age now where you must make the best decision for you. Whatever that is, I support you. I wish only to see you as happy every day as you are here."

I blinked away tears as I stared up into my father's face. "Being here is my heaven," I admitted. "This is my choice of where to live permanently once school is finished. She will have no say anymore since I will be an adult."

I could see how upset he was. Not for himself, but for me.

"I do not like my little girl feeling trapped. If you want out mi ángel, you say that. I will fight for you. Your mother can deal with me."

I leaned in and kissed his cheek. "I love that you are always my warrior, Papá."

The party was in full swing and we were all having a wonderful time. In Spain the legal drinking age is eighteen, so the boys had hoped everyone would be allowed to drink since we were right on top of being legal. Since we'd turned sixteen, our parents regularly permitted us to drink cava or sangria with dinner. The twins had been sure that meant they'd be cool with letting us have wine and some flavored punch for our friends, but it was a no-go. While they felt confident that the three of us knew our limits, they couldn't say the same about Dio and Rafe's friends.

The twins were let down, but I didn't see it as a loss. I enjoyed the taste of some wines, but beer was gross and most sweet flavored alcohol made me gag. Plus, if I wanted a glass of sangria or cava, all I had to do was go into the house to drink it with our parents.

In the yard people were spread out into several groups. There was a group playing ping-pong, a big bunch of kids in the pool and still another crowd was sitting around the pool listening to music. Everything was going along smoothly until Rafe's girlfriend, Francesca, showed up. She was overly sensitive and prone to dramatic fits that put my nerves on edge. Dio detested her, as did Joaquin. They tried to talk to him but it wasn't like Rafe listened.

Any time one of us so much as said boo about Francesca, he got mad and said we were wrong about her. I didn't think we were—and her showing up with a trunk full of vodka and rum that she'd bribed a busboy from her parents' restaurant to buy for her was another reason not to like her. Antonio and Camila had been very clear— but Francesca had no respect for them, probably because she'd never met them. Rafe looked uncomfortable that she'd brought alcohol, but he didn't tell her to knock it off.

Dio, Joaquin and I all chose not to drink any of what Francesca had arrived with. Dio might have been disappointed when his parents said they wouldn't provide alcohol, but he was still respectful. They'd said no. To him, that was that. Joaquin didn't drink because he had to be in top form at all times for fútbol. I was impressed by his devotion to his dream. I often wished I felt drawn to something as passionately. So far, I was clueless about what I wanted to do in college. Would I go for business? Design? Maybe I'd go to nursing school. I honestly had no idea. The only thing I knew for certain was that I wanted Spain to be my real home base.

As the party wore on and most people were getting tipsy if not downright drunk, I was finding the whole thing less and less enjoyable. Francesca was being ridiculous, flouncing around giving Rafe tons of attitude and grief, outright yelling at him several times. Not to mention, she was hanging on a few of our guy friends, one in particular. I wasn't sure why Rafe wasn't calling her out, to be honest. Just watching her behave the way she was, made me uncomfortable. I put up with it for as long as I could, but once she turned her attention my way, I needed a reprieve. Leaving Dio and Joaquin in the yard to keep an eye on things, I headed into the house in search of some quiet. I could hear the adults in the Cruz's game room, likely playing poker. My father and Antonio loved the game, and Camila enjoyed going head-to-head with them as well.

Exhausted by Francesca's antics, I decided to take a few minutes to relax and enjoy the silence. Hungry for something sweet, I lifted the domed lid off the counter dessert display, pulled out a crème filled pastry and set it down on a dessert plate before crossing the room to the coffee bar where I prepared myself an Americano. I'd just started to relax when I heard Francesca start screeching. Letting out a sigh, I set my half-eaten pastry down and stood from the counter. Not wanting her to see me looking, lest it cause yet another dramatic outburst, I quietly made my way through the kitchen and out to the sunroom. The lights were off, allowing me to position myself in the shadows so I could see and hear what was happening without detection.

By then Francesca was in full snit, her hands flailing as she bitched Rafe out. It took me a minute to discern the cause of her latest eruption, but when I did, I rolled my damn eyes. She was railing at him for telling her to quiet down so his parents didn't come to see what was happening. Clearly she hadn't taken his pleas to heart because her screeching was at an all-time high. Personally, I thought she needed to have her filthy mouth washed out with soap, and my hands went to my hips as I considered going outside and getting into it with her. The girl was garbage and something needed to be done. I shook it off by reminding myself that confronting her while my father, Antonio and Camila were in the house would open a can of worms and I wouldn't do that to the boys.

I felt bad for Rafe but was also frustrated that he was taking her abuse. I knew if she kept it up his parents would absolutely overhear and wind up in the yard to see what was happening—and at that point he was going to be in a shitload of trouble because it was obvious people were drinking. It also wouldn't be an ideal way for them to meet Francesca but I thought maybe that could be a good thing. Realizing there was nothing I could do, I sighed and shook my head as I turned to retreat to the kitchen.

When I turned, I saw a man in the doorway watching me. I gasped as he stepped into the darkened room with a masculine grace that was magnetizing—so much so that I naturally took a few steps forward. I came to an abrupt halt when I realized the man walking toward me was Mateo Cruz, who I hadn't seen in over a year. During that time he'd somehow changed. I'd never been attracted to him before but it felt like I was seeing him with new eyes. He was gorgeous.

How had I never noticed before? I was flustered and completely flummoxed by my reaction to him. Out of all the Cruz boys, it had only ever been Alejandro I'd found attractive to me personally. Right then I couldn't remember why I'd ever thought Mateo wasn't the most beautiful man in the world.

"Mateo," I said breathlessly as I stared up into his green eyes, "you scared the life out of me. You're home early."

His head reared back as his eyebrows shot up in surprise.

"*Avelina*?"

I chuckled nervously and bit my lip as I stared up at him. "Yep. I guess you didn't recognize me?"

His gaze raked over me from head to toe before they came back to my face. Several seconds ticked off before he shook his head, almost like he was coming out of a trance.

"Not from behind," he admitted.

"I grew two whole inches since I saw you last," I boasted with a little laugh. At five foot seven, I wasn't ever going to be model height.

Mateo raked a hand through his hair and let out a harsh laugh. "Yes," he murmured, "that must be it. Your father says you are about to start your final year of school. You are the same age as the twins, right? That makes you…"

"They're a little younger than I am," I reminded him. "I'll be eighteen before they are."

"Cristo," he said huskily, "eres tan joven."

"I'm not that young," I countered. "In two short months, I'll be an adult."

Never had I wanted so badly to be older.

He made a dismissive gesture with his hand as he shook his head. "I did not mean to offend," he assured me.

I knew it hadn't been his intention, but for some reason, his thinking of me as a child rubbed me the wrong way. Before I could say a word about it, the glass door that led out to the yard was flung open noisily.

"No!" Francesca screeched angrily. "Get off of me, Rafe! That puta needs to be spoken to!"

I stiffened as I turned and saw a very disheveled looking Rafe attempting to hold Francesca back as she hissed like a wet cat and tried to dislodge him.

"Come on, Chess," he pleaded, "you're just drunk."

"No! I'm not. I know you and your brothers have been fucking her and I will stop it!"

It was obvious she was talking about me. My jaw dropped as I gaped at her, completely done with her insanity. I'd been nothing but nice to her, and she'd just stepped over a line.

"Excuse me?" I snapped as I stepped toward her. "Are you serious?"

My head reared back when she spit at me, a shower of it landing on the floor in front of me. I was normally levelheaded and willing to put up with a lot in the hopes of keeping things from escalating, but she'd gone too far. Anger boiled in my veins as I raised a hand to slap her.

Before I could connect, I was jerked back against a hard body as Mateo wrapped his arms around me and pulled me away from her.

"Get this psycho out of our house before I slap her myself," Mateo barked at Rafe.

"Who the fuck do you think you're calling a psycho?" Francesca sputtered drunkenly.

Mateo didn't get to answer because our parents burst into the room from one direction while Diego and Joaquin came through the same door behind Rafe and Francesca. The overhead light went on, taking the room out of the shadows. With the room no longer bathed in darkness, it was even more apparent that Francesca was a drunken mess. Her hair was all over the place and her eyes had that droopy look people took on when they were blitzed.

"What in the hell is going on here?" Antonio thundered.

Any normal person would've known to stop at that point. Antonio was a large and imposing figure, and his voice was full of authority. His arrival should've diffused the situation, but Francesca wasn't having it.

"Great, it's the parents," she slurred. "What's going on is your sons are fucking this ugly tramp like she's the town dump!"

Papá, Antonio and Camila looked absolutely thunderstruck. Camila sputtered as Antonio stepped forward. My father grabbed his arm and stopped him with a curse.

"Who is this trash speaking to my daughter this way?" he bellowed.

I'd never seen him so angry. His face was red and he

was shaking as he glared at Francesca. I wiggled out of Mateo's arms and hurried to my father.

"It's okay, Papá. Nothing she said is true and it doesn't matter. She's just drunk."

"No! I won't have you spoken to like that. Not here, not anywhere. This is unacceptable."

"I've got this Quino," Antonio assured my father as he crossed the room to Francesca and Rafe.

"*This* is your girlfriend?" he asked.

Rafe nodded. "She's just drunk—"

"And rude," Antonio said harshly. "I want her gone from my home. She is not welcome here, not now, not ever. I'm calling your parents," he snapped at Francesca. "You should be ashamed of yourself."

"I'm not. You don't get to judge me," she slurred.

"Then you should behave like a proper young lady. What you have done here is shameful."

Francesca finally seemed to clue in that she'd gone too far. She deflated under Antonio's angry gaze, slumping against Rafe's side.

"I'm sorry, Papá," Rafe said quietly.

"Sí," Antonio said stiffly. "You most assuredly will be sorry. You're grounded for the rest of the summer and you will apologize to Avelina. I'm ashamed of you for letting this trash talk to her like that."

I felt awful for Rafe, even though he'd brought some of it on himself by not shutting Francesca down when she showed up with alcohol.

Turning to Diego and Joaquin, Antonio instructed them to end the party and have anyone who hadn't been drinking go home. Everyone else would either be driven home by security or would spend the night out in the guest casita. My attention was on his orders when everything went to hell. Suddenly my father grabbed his chest and made a sound I knew I'd hear in my nightmares forever.

I let out a frantic scream as he dropped to his knees, his eyes wide and desperate as he looked at me.

"Papá!" I yelled.

He made a choked sound as he shook his head. "Mi ángel," he gasped.

Mateo jumped into action, grabbing my father to steady him before looking up at Camila.

"Call for an ambulance!"

Everything was pandemonium as everyone in the room freaked out. In the blink of an eye some of the security team burst into the room. I shook like a leaf, unable to move. Antonio wrapped his arms around me to hold me in place as Mateo and Antonio's head security guard took care of my father. Papá's coloring went from bad to worse as each moment passed. I swayed on my feet when Mateo began performing CPR, the edges of my vision turning black as I watched. I gulped in a lungful of air, forcing myself to stay upright and alert.

Things felt worse to me when the ambulance arrived and they took over. Instead of announcing that everything was going to be fine, which I'd been praying for, they sprang into action and told us all to step back. I let out a shriek as they cut off my dad's shirt to use the defibrillator. Suddenly Mateo was right at my side, pulling me out of his father's arms. I cried against his chest as he held me tight.

Only his strength kept me upright.

# Five

*Four Years Ago*

THE HOSPITAL WAITING ROOM WAS ALMOST church-like in its silence. My father had gone in the ambulance while Antonio, Mateo and I were driven right behind it by security. Camila initially had no choice but to stay behind to make sure Francesca's parents came to get her and also to ensure no one who shouldn't be driving left the house. She'd gotten to the hospital two hours later, having left Rafe and Dio at home to clean up the mess. Poor Joaquin had been left in charge to supervise.

Since I was still a minor, Antonio was technically in charge. After Valeria had died, my father had assigned him power of attorney. When I was fifteen he had added an addendum stating that in case of emergency all decisions had to be approved by me, but until I was eighteen Antonio had to be the one to give permission for anything to be done. When we'd first arrived, he'd signed a series of papers to approve any and all measures to save my father.

Not too long later, a surgeon came and told us my father had suffered a massive heart attack and he needed to undergo emergency bypass surgery.

The minutes passed like years as we waited for word, and as every tick of the clock went by without any, my anxiety grew exponentially. All I could do, all any of us could do, was pray that he would survive the surgery. Nothing was guaranteed and thinking of my father on a heart-lung bypass machine terrified me. What if something went wrong? What if he didn't survive? My father was everything to me, the most solid part of my entire world. We hadn't had enough time together. I wanted him at my side for many, many years to come.

It was almost dawn when the surgeon we'd spoken to previously, Dr. Garcia, finally stepped into the room to speak to us, panic raced through my veins. Was he going to be the bearer of bad news? I think my heart skipped a dozen beats as he crossed the room toward us. Only when he smiled at me encouragingly did I remember to breathe. Antonio held my left hand and Mateo held my right when the doctor sat down across from us.

"Mr. Saez made it through surgery without complication. He's being moved to the cardiac intensive care unit, where you will be able to see him later today."

"Later?" I squeaked. "Why not now?"

"The patient must be given time to rest," he explained. "I know it is hard, but trust me when I tell you his body needs this time. So does yours, I am certain. Get some sleep and come back this afternoon."

My shoulders sagged as I nodded and let out a long sigh. When Mateo squeezed my hand encouragingly, I found myself leaning against him. As much as I loved and adored Antonio, it was Mateo who was keeping me tethered to reality. I couldn't explain why, but I needed him at my side.

"How many visitors will be allowed at a time?" Antonio asked.

I was glad he did since I hadn't thought to. It was good that someone was on the ball. I definitely wasn't.

"The hospital policy is two at a time," Dr. Garcia responded. "We ask that you have anyone who is ill refrain from visiting. It's vital that we keep ICU areas as sterile as possible."

As he was speaking the weight of the preceding hours hit me hard. I'd been awake for twenty hours and right then, I could feel it. Not long after the doctor left the waiting room, we were all making our way out of the hospital. I felt like I was in a daze as I shook the doctor's hand and thanked him for taking care of my father. Antonio and Camila held hands as they walked alongside Mateo and me. He seemed to know that I wasn't as steady as I could be, so he'd put his arm over my shoulders, holding me protectively against his side as he guided me toward the car. Since Camila had come separately, there were two SUV's at the curb waiting for us. It was decided that she and Antonio would go in one and Mateo and I would go in the other.

I was numb as Mateo and I climbed into the back of the vehicle. Once the guard closed the door behind him, Mateo turned and assessed me. "You must put on your safety belt, Avelina."

I frowned when I realized I hadn't. It was second

nature to me to put it on the instant I was seated since my father had always been a stickler about it. The thought of my father instantly gave way to the memory of him lying on the floor not breathing. My hands shook as I tried to belt myself in, but I was too unsteady to get the belt into the slot. Mateo came to my rescue, his warm fingers covering mine as he helped me click it into place. Unable to hold it in any longer, I let out a choked sob. I was terrified and I couldn't pretend otherwise.

Mateo unbelted himself and slid across the seat so that he was right next to me before wrapping his arms around me.

"I'm s-s-sorry," I wailed.

"Do not be sorry."

I clutched his shirt as I cried against his chest. Great body-racking sobs consumed me as I replayed the events over and over in my mind. My father, the person I loved most in the world, had almost died.

"Lean on me and let it all out," he murmured as he placed a tissue in my hand.

I wiped my nose but his shirt continued to catch all of my tears as I leaned against him while he rubbed his hand up and down my back soothingly.

"Quino is going to be okay," he assured me. "He is strong."

I cried harder even as I nodded. Before his collapse, I'd seen my father as invincible. He wasn't just a man to me; he was a superhero. A father who didn't ever give up and who never missed a milestone, he'd always had my back no matter what. Seeing him near death on the floor had rocked me to my core.

I stayed in Mateo's arms while he held me and let me cry until I had no more tears left. Even after I was finished, I didn't move away. Instead, I held tight and listened to the pounding of his heart beneath my ear.

When we got back to the villa, and I got out of the car, he lifted me into his arms and carried me inside, asking me for directions to my bedroom as he walked. After turning on the light, he set me down on the bed and crouched down in front of me.

"What do you need?" he asked.

I wasn't sure he would agree to what I needed.

My pulse raced as I bit the bullet and went for it. "Will you stay with me until I fall asleep?"

His eyes widened before his expression softened. "Of course."

I got up from the bed and went into my closet where I took off my dress—the one I'd been so excited about hours before but now knew I'd never wear again—and pulled on my cotton nightdress and a long robe.

When I got back into my bedroom, I found Mateo sitting on my swivel chair studying the photo board above my desk. He kept his back to me as I climbed into bed and got under the covers.

"Did you take all of these photos?" he asked as he turned to face me.

"Other than the ones I'm in, yes."

He gestured to the photos behind my bed, a collection of pictures I'd taken in Spain over the course of the previous few years. "Including those?"

I nodded.

"You have an amazing eye."

It wasn't entirely joyous, but his words brought my first real smile since my father collapsed.

"Thank you."

He nodded and pointed to the light next to my bed. "You should turn that off and go to sleep," he said. "I will stay right here and watch over you."

I frowned and looked away as I twisted a piece of my comforter between my fingers.

"What is wrong?" he asked.

What was wrong was that I wanted him closer.

I looked back to him nervously. "I… can you sit up here on the bed next to me?"

He glanced away and cleared his throat before nodding. "Whatever you need."

We watched each other silently as he got up from the chair and crossed the room to me.

He gestured down to the empty space next to me. "Here?"

I nodded as he kicked off his shoes and got onto the bed next to me where he settled on top of the covers and propped himself up with a pillow against the headboard.

Just having him close like that somehow calmed me. I yawned and rolled to my side so I would be facing him. My eyes began to droop as I stared at him.

"Thank you for this," I murmured. "I know it's a lot to have asked for."

He shook his head as he reached out and brushed a strand of hair off my forehead.

"There is nothing you could ask for that I would not give you."

When he went to pull his hand back, I reached up

and took it in mine. I fell asleep just like that.

When I woke up four hours later, he was gone. I'd slept so soundly that I hadn't heard him leave. I had a text message from Antonio telling me that my father was resting comfortably. He said he'd get back to me as soon as he spoke to the doctor and we had the all clear to visit.

After a stop in the kitchen to make myself a tea, I headed back into my room. I opened my curtains and slid the doors to my patio apart. Taking a seat at my small café table, I drank my tea slowly, trying to delay the inevitable. Once the last sip was gone, I picked up the phone and called my mother.

Naturally, her reaction to my news was less than enthusiastic.

"I can't understand why your father's health scare would have any effect on your schooling. You attend one of the most prestigious private schools in New York City and you're going into your senior year. I won't allow it, Lina. This is ridiculous. Your father should be ashamed of himself for manipulating you this way."

My teeth ground together as she spoke. I absolutely detested the way she refused to call me anything but Lina. I was not, nor had I ever been, a Lina. My mother didn't care. She thought Avelina was "too Spanish sounding" and Ava was "too common." Therefore, she had called me Lina, which she said was exotic and unusual, since I was in middle school. Even knowing how much I hated it, she refused to back down.

"Papá didn't have a heart attack to manipulate me,"

I bit out. "Knock it off. You know what you just said is ridiculous and if you talk about him like that again, I'm going to hang up. Whether you like him or not he's my father, the only one I'll ever have. He's been the best parent I could ever have asked for and I adore him. When you insult him, you're insulting me."

"Stop with the histrionics," she answered bitterly. "I know you're daddy's little girl, but throwing away your future—"

"I've made the decision. It's done."

"It isn't done, Lina. You forget that you're a minor," she said triumphantly.

Tears rolled unchecked down my cheeks as I cried silently. It was awful to have her arguing with me at a time when all I could think about were the events of the night before. Over and over again in my mind's eye I saw my father clutching his chest and collapsing, a nightmare on a never-ending loop. Swiping the tears away, I forced myself to breathe.

"I'm well aware of how old I am," I sniffled. "I'm *also* aware that if you push this and it winds up in court, the judge will rule in my favor. I'm almost eighteen, Mother. I get a say in my future and this is what I want. It's up to you how to handle it—you can create a scene or accept it, but at the end of the day, it's done. I'm here and I'm not leaving."

"You're too much like him," she gritted. "You act like Spain is the be all and end all, but it's not."

"Neither is New York City," I answered stiffly. "This really isn't that difficult. It's what I want and if you care for me the way you say you do, you'll support me."

"You'll do what you want whether I do or not. I see I have no choice but don't expect me to be happy about it. You can also tell your father that this doesn't affect his monthly payments. Our agreement says he's to pay me every month until you're out of college. If I'm shorted by even a dollar, I'm taking him to court."

I winced at her words, mortified that she was making it about money. It was always that way with her and I was uncomfortable about it. Before I could respond she hung up without another word. I pulled the phone away from my ear and stared at it blankly for several moments before I fumbled it back into its spot on my bedside table. I felt queasy and unsettled, which was par for the course after anything to do with money was brought up. I'd never been able to wrap my mind around the obscene amount of money my father gave her, particularly since I spent so much of my time with him.

A few years before I'd overheard Antonio scolding my father for not taking my mother to court. Listening to that conversation was how I found out that not only did Papá own the New York apartment my mother and I lived in, he paid for my tuition himself and still gave her a hundred thousand dollars a month in child support. This was in addition to cutting her checks any time she told him she needed extra for me. She'd gotten three million dollars when she left him, even though they'd never been married and she did not have a right to his money. I knew this because I'd heard her crowing about it to her friends before. Realizing she was still taking him for money had made me sick to my stomach.

Logically, I knew that just over a million dollars a year

in support was nothing to my father, but it didn't matter. It was obscene to me that she got what she did since it was always my dad who paid for everything. All of my clothes, my computer, my cellphone, even the groceries in my mother's apartment were delivered weekly by Papá's New York housekeeper. I couldn't remember a time when my mother had bought me anything that wasn't a Christmas or birthday gift and even those I suspected were provided by him.

I slumped against my headboard with a harsh exhale. I'd been so foolish to stay in New York with my mother. When I turned fourteen, the courts would have factored in my wishes—but I'd allowed her to manipulate me into being a good girl. Had I just stuck to my guns and come to live in Spain, as I had wanted to do, my father would have been better cared for. Maybe without the constant travel back and forth to visit me or the stress of dealing with my mother, his health wouldn't have suffered.

My reverie came to a halt when I heard a knock at my bedroom door. The guards would not come up to the second floor unless there was a commotion or one of the panic buttons was pushed, so I figured it was Antonio or Camila coming to discuss when we would go to the hospital.

I crossed the room quickly and opened the door, surprised when I found myself face to face with Mateo. His large frame towered above me as he smiled warmly.

"My father sent me over to tell you he just got off the phone with the doctor—Quino is doing well. He'd like to go to the hospital in about an hour."

I breathed a sigh of relief as I threw myself against

him impulsively, wrapping my arms around him in a hug.

"Oh thank God," I squeaked. "I've been so anxious for information."

As Mateo hugged me back, I basked in this scent of his cologne. When I pressed my cheek against his firm chest so I could breathe him as covertly as possible, he let out a choked sound and stepped back like he'd been scalded.

"You should dress," he rasped.

I glanced down at myself and was immediately embarrassed to realize I'd taken my robe off. This meant I was clad only in one of my short white cotton nightgowns. Although it landed just below my thighs, it was super virginal looking. I felt myself blush as I crossed my arms uncomfortably. I must have looked like such a fool.

My heart beat funny in my chest as I looked back up at him. His green eyes studied me as I fidgeted nervously.

"I'll get ready and come over in a few minutes," I said.

He nodded as he took a step back, his eyes dropping down to my legs before he quickly looked up to my face again.

"I will see you there," he answered before he spun on his heel and hastily walked away.

I was happy to see my father sitting up in bed even though he looked very pale and fragile to me. His voice was a hoarse whisper, his throat sore from having been intubated. Because of his incision, I was not able to hug him, so we held hands as I choked back tears and told him how much I loved him. He squeezed my fingers encouragingly as he assured me he wasn't going anywhere and would take better care of himself.

Papá lit up when I told him that I would be staying in Spain to finish out my senior year of high school at the American School of Barcelona. We talked it out with Antonio and it was agreed that Camila would register me there immediately.

When he asked me how my mother took the news, I told him she had been fine. He quirked an eyebrow and gave me a dubious look that made me laugh. My father was no fool, which meant he knew perfectly well she'd given me what for. But he also knew I was as stubborn and determined as he was.

Antonio and I stayed at the hospital with Papá until well after dark. We agreed that I would be allowed to stay in the house by myself until he came home from the hospital. Antonio and Camila would be in charge while he was gone, which was not a problem since I saw them every day anyway.

We left the hospital just before seven at night after my father admitted that he was very tired and needed to rest. I hadn't really eaten all day so by the time we got home I was ravenous. Camila had made a big dinner and there were leftovers for me to eat which was a blessing. When we got into the house, Rafe and Mateo were talking in the kitchen. Rafe bounded over to me and gave me a big hug.

"I'm so sorry about last night," he said, his voice trembling with emotion. "I love Tío Quino and I was devastated by what happened. I'm so glad he's okay," he sniffled. "You have every right to be mad, but I hope you'll forgive me."

I sighed and dropped a kiss on his cheek.

"I'm not mad at you," I emphasized, "but I *am* angry. The way Francesca acted was crazy and completely out of control. I realize what happened to my father would have happened anyway at some point, but it didn't need to happen that way."

He nodded as I stepped out of his arms and looked him over.

"The way she spoke to me was not okay and I'm not going to let that go. To be totally honest, I don't think you should take it either. She talks to everyone like that because she isn't a nice person. Last night wasn't the first instance of her having a tantrum or speaking to people like they're dirt. That's not normal and you deserve better."

Antonio stood quietly while I had my say but when I finish speaking he put his hand on Rafe's shoulder and looked him in the eye.

"You will not see that girl again," he said, his voice offering no leeway. "She is trash and I will not have that in my home or around my family. Spending time with people like that is not how your mama and I raised you. Francesca is nothing but trouble and I won't have that hurting my family again."

Rafe's shoulders sagged as he looked down at the floor dejectedly.

"I swear she's not normally like that," he said. "You didn't meet the real her."

I understood Rafe wanting to defend her, but he was lying. She was always like that. Perhaps she was slightly less dramatic on a daily basis but not by much. I'd met the real her dozens of times and I couldn't stand her.

"Alcohol brings things to the surface," Antonio said. "What you saw last night was the real her. Don't you stand here and defend her nonsense, son. I've already spoken with your brothers and both have told me that she is very dramatic. Do not let her ruin your life, Rafe. Your mother and I will not allow it."

Mateo had been standing by the whole time, arms crossed across his broad chest, not saying a word. He watched us closely, monitoring the situation. After Antonio said for the second time that they wouldn't allow Rafe to see her anymore, Mateo nodded his head in approval.

"He is right, Rafe," Mateo offered. "You should never accept that kind of treatment. A girl who would disrespect the rules of your parents and speak to and about an extended family member the way she did is not acceptable. She was rude to your family, brother. That is unforgivable."

"Her parents are very hard on her and it has made her—" Rafe began.

"It is not a negotiation," Antonio said firmly. "She is not welcome in my home and you are forbidden to see her. If I find out you've disobeyed, there will be consequences."

Personally, I couldn't understand why Rafe was defending her at all. Francesca wasn't a nice person. It was like everybody else saw it but he had blinders on where she was concerned. It didn't make sense. Dio had joked before that Rafe was pussy whipped. More and more I was coming to realize he was right. Rafe had lost his virginity to her and I think it made him overly accepting of her crappy behavior.

The conversation ended there. Antonio went to go talk to Camila and tell her about our day with my father at the hospital while the rest of us stayed back in the kitchen. Not too long later Dio and Joaquin joined us while I was heating up food. Camila had made fried eggplant with an olive tapenade and a side of pasta, all of which I practically inhaled, along with three large helpings of crusty bread. As I ate, the boys peppered me with questions.

They were so excited for me to finally be living where I chose to. It was what I had always wanted. I wasn't nervous about it at all because I knew a bunch of their friends, which meant I wouldn't have a weird case of first day jitters. While we were on the subject of school, Mateo asked me where I intended to go to college.

"I'll stay here and go to the University of Barcelona since it was always my intention anyway. I've always wanted to live here full-time."

Mateo nodded before setting his chin down on his hand. "Quino speaks often about your love for all things Spain. Your roots here are thick. It is good to feel so connected to something."

"What about you?" I asked. "What's your plan now that you're finished at Harvard? Will you move home immediately to start at Cruz Saez headquarters?"

He shook his head in the negative. "Not just yet. I have taken a job with the largest grocery chain on the east coast. Technically they are our competitors, but our fathers are close with the owner. His son and daughter both worked at Cruz Saez when they came out of college. Doing it this way will help blunt any claim of nepotism when I join CS permanently," he explained. "My father and yours are encouraging all of us to take that route. It will be a temporary job—just two years from start to finish."

"You just want to stay in America because the babes are so damn fine," Joaquin joked. "I've seen your smoking hot girlfriends. "

Mateo flushed, his eyes darting to me before quickly moving away. "Sometimes, Joaquin, you talk like an idiot. "

"Nah," Joaquin laughed. "You know I'm right, you're just embarrassed because there's a girl at the table. "

"He's right," Dio said. "You're surrounded by so many beautiful girls it's sickening. I've stalked your Facebook and seen the chicks you go to school with. It's why I added Harvard to my list. It can't hurt to be surrounded by foxes. And never be embarrassed to say things in front of Ava. She's one of the guys."

"You are a fool," Mateo said dryly. "Avelina is no guy. Show some respect. I am sure she does not want to hear about girls you think are beautiful."

It was sweet the way he defended me. I also enjoyed the way Mateo spoke more formally than his brothers. This was because he'd learned English only as a second language at school until he was fourteen and moved in with his father. His brothers had always gone to American schools and spoke both languages fluently.

"The only one of us she would be even a little upset about is Alejandro," Dio joked. "He's the only Cruz she's ever had eyes for."

My face felt like it was on fire. Mateo's face seemed frozen in shock for several seconds before he frowned.

"Is that true?" he asked gruffly. "Do you like Alejandro?"

I shook my head emphatically. "No," I said firmly.

Joaquin cackled. "You used to trail along after him like a puppy."

I made a mental note to strangle him at a later date.

"Used to being the operative words in that sentence," I argued. "I grew out of my silly Alejandro crush years ago."

"It's true," Rafe laughed. "Right before high school started she stopped caring. He could waltz in here with Kate Upton tomorrow and Ava wouldn't care."

"Dude, you suck," Dio laughed. "Obviously she doesn't like him anymore, but that doesn't mean we can't tease her about it. She teases us about everything. It's our job to torture her."

"Be nice to Avelina," Mateo growled.

"You should call her Ava," Rafe announced.

"I have not been invited to do so," Mateo said as he looked to me. "Would you prefer that?"

I wanted him to call me whatever he wanted, just so I could hear his voice more often. "My friends call me Ava, the family calls me Avelina. I answer to both."

"Now that we are friends and not just extended family, I will call you both."

"As long as you never, ever call me Lina, it's fine," I chuckled.

The boys all laughed, knowing how much I detested my mother's chosen nickname for me. Mateo wrinkled his nose and cocked his head. "Lina? That is one I have not heard you called before."

I rolled my eyes. "My mother refuses to call me

anything else, even though she knows I hate it."

"And yet she named you Avelina," Mateo pointed out.

"Papá's mother was named Avelina and he felt strongly about naming me after her," I explained. "My mother apparently has always hated the name. She says Avelina is too Spanish and Ava is too common, so she refuses to call me either."

He was frowning as I finished speaking.

"She sounds charming," he said stiffly. "I find myself glad not to have crossed paths with her."

"She's definitely an acquired taste," I conceded.

"Ava's too nice. Her mom is a straight up bitch," Rafe opined.

I wasn't surprised. The boys loathed my mother and always had. I couldn't fault them for it. Anytime they came to New York and saw her in the building my father kept an apartment in, she was rude to them. They also knew plenty about the hoops she made my father jump through.

"Watch your mouth when there is a woman present," Mateo snapped.

"We told you, Ava is one of the guys," Dio snorted.

"I'm so used to it I don't even notice anymore," I assured Mateo.

"See?" Dio laughed. "She's cool. She doesn't mind the way we talk and she just laughs I tell her I'm going to go to college in America to meet hot chicks. She knows all our secrets and we know hers. Stop being so uptight."

Mateo rolled his eyes. "I am not uptight," he argued. "I was merely saying you should not choose a school because what the student body looks like. Besides, if beauty is what you are in search of there is plenty of it right here in Spain," he said as his eyes quickly darted to me before settling on the table.

My mouth felt desert dry. Had Mateo just hinted that he found me beautiful? No, I chided myself, that couldn't be it. Exhaustion was making me loopy. I leaned back in my chair and let out a yawn.

"I'm really tired," I announced drowsily. "I'm going to go home, take a shower, check my email and go to bed."

"Yeah, you need to sleep," Dio said. "Are you sure you don't want one of us to spend the night with you? It's gotta be weird being over there alone. We can drag the guestroom beds into your room like we used to do when we were kids. Slumber party at Ava's!"

I waved him off. "You're nuts. If you want to take a trip down memory lane, I'm up for a slumber party at a later date, but right now I'm too exhausted to even function. After my shower, I'm going to crawl into bed and pass out in about five seconds. Don't worry about me— It's not like I'm alone since there are always two guards in the house," I reminded him as I stood, carrying my dishes from the table to the sink.

Rafe, Dio and Joaquin each hugged me goodbye, leaving only Mateo behind. He stood at the counter and watched as I rinsed my dishes and put them in the dishwasher.

"I will walk you home," he announced as I dried my hands on a soft sage colored kitchen towel.

I felt guilty for taking up so much of his time. "You don't have to," I assured him. "It's so close—"

He shook his head. "I am walking you home," he said

firmly.

The night was warm, the air fragrant with the scent of the citrus trees, carnations, bougainvillea, roses and gazanias that were planted throughout both of our properties. I found myself wishing I'd put more thought into my outfit. Clad in navy shorts, a white tee shirt and a pair of white Adidas sneakers, I wouldn't be winning any awards for my attire. Mateo was dressed simply too, a pair of khaki colored cargo shorts and a black tee shirt, but he looked amazing. I felt sloppy, especially with my hair up in a messy bun. I'd gone from not thinking of Mateo much at all to wanting to impress him.

"You are very quiet," he noted as he looked over at me with concern. "Are you doing okay?"

I blushed, embarrassed because the reason I was being quiet was entirely because of my newly acquired attraction to him.

"I'm fine, just a little tired," I hastily assured him. "I didn't get to sleep for very long last night and it's really catching up to me now."

Mateo nodded at the security guard who was stationed outside as we made our way to my front door. I entered the code and cracked the door open before turning and looking up at him. His eyes captivated me, the green reminding me of the emerald ocean along the Canary Islands. In some lights his eyes were light, in others they were as dark as any emerald I'd ever seen.

"Did your mother have green eyes?" I blurted.

He looked surprised. "She did. Why do you ask?"

I felt myself blush as I bit my lip and looked away. "Your father and brothers all have blue eyes," I answered.

"It just dawned on me you must take after your mother."

He smiled softly. "Sí. Mi madre tenía hermosos ojos verdes."

He'd said his mother had beautiful green eyes, and warmth spread through my veins because of the emotion behind his words. I could tell he loved her.

"You miss her," I said. It wasn't a question—it was an observation.

Mateo nodded. "Everyday. I understand my father will always be angry about her choice, but I cannot find it in my heart to feel anything but love for her. She was a strong woman, a beautiful soul. Madre was always there for me. No one is a saint. She made decisions I wish she had not, but I love her just the same. Being mad at the dead is a waste of time. When we meet in the afterlife, I will ask her why she did things the way she did. Until then, I will focus on the happy memories."

I'd never realized how mature Mateo was before.

"I bet she would be proud of how well you've turned out," I said.

He smiled then, so dazzlingly that even with the cloak of night surrounding us, I felt like I was near the sun.

"I like to think so. My father does not like to speak of her, but many things I do are based on lessons she taught me. It means a lot for you to say that, Avelina."

I had to look down so as not to get lost in his eyes again.

"I know we've not really spoken much before, so you being there for me last night was really above and beyond," I said, my voice trembling with emotion. "Without you, Papá might not have made it until the ambulance arrived. I appreciate everything you did for him and I owe you one for letting me lose it the way I did on the way home in the car."

I startled when he traced along the side of my cheek with his finger. "You owe me nothing because I wanted to be here with you," he assured me.

"I'm grateful," I answered, "and my father will be delighted when I tell him everything you did."

"Your father has always meant a lot to me."

I smiled as I looked up at him. "You mean a lot to him, too," I answered. "Between you and me, I know you're his favorite. Sometimes I tease him that he'd trade me for you."

His finger dropped from my cheek as he let out a choked laugh. "No one in their right mind would *ever* trade you for anyone or anything else."

The air around us felt thicker as we stared at each other. For one brief moment I thought he might kiss me. I licked my lips and took half a step forward, only to feel foolish when he took two steps back.

"You should go to bed," he said.

I stepped back and walked through the open door in the hopes he wouldn't see the disappointed look on my face.

"Yes," I agreed as I leaned against the frame. "I should. I'm sure you're exhausted, too."

He shrugged. "Not so tired that I will not be right here if you need anything or you decide you would rather not stay here. Just call the house and I will come right over."

"Thank you, Mateo."

When he smiled down at me, I forgot to breathe for

several seconds. He grinned as he turned away.

"Dulce Sueños," he called back over his shoulder.

That night I fell asleep replaying those few seconds when I'd thought Mateo was going to kiss me over in my mind. What would it take to get him to actually do it?

# *Six*

I SUCKED IN A BREATH WHEN I OPENED THE DOOR AND saw the master bedroom had been redone, too. A massive black four-poster bed with cream bedding had replaced the previous cherry wood sleigh bed.

I was relieved Mateo hadn't followed me into the room because I could not contain my gasp of wonder as I looked around and drank in the way the room had turned out. The furniture was black with brushed chrome accents and there were mirrored side tables on either side of the bed. I'd worked hard on the entire apartment, but the bedroom had been the most time consuming. The decorating consultant I'd worked with had found four different custom furniture designers and I'd gone with the one who had the most dynamic pieces. The end result was even better than I'd imagined.

My mouth went dry as I turned and realized that there was a large collage of photos hanging over the sitting area. I stepped forward tentatively, surprised to see that all of the photos were of the two of us together. It was not something I'd put together, which meant Mateo had. My eyes filled with tears as I came to a stop in front of the display. Anyone looking at the collage would believe they were looking at a couple madly in love. To be sure it was what I had believed over the years as the photos were taken. I forced myself to turn my back on the display of photos and walk away because it hurt too much to see all I'd lost.

The view on Mateo's side of the bed was no better. My stomach dropped when I saw the photos of me he'd always kept there. There were two images in the frame, a reminder of something special to both of us. Both pictures were of just my face, taken to mark the once-in-a-lifetime occasion. I remembered Mateo above me, taking the first photo before and the next one just after we'd made love. I blushed crimson as I picked up the frame and stared at that younger version of myself. It was obvious the photos had been taken at an intimate time. In the first, I looked needy and aroused, and in the second, I looked sated and joyful. I bit the inside of my cheek as I set the frame down and turned it away so I wouldn't have to look at it.

My breath started coming faster as anxiety raced through my veins. I couldn't stay in the apartment all day doing nothing because it would drive me nuts. Needing something to do, I decided I'd spend some time in the pool on the terrace. Until I calmed down enough to talk to him, I needed to avoid him like the plague. That meant denial was the order of the day.

I made my way into the master bath where I opened the door to the closet, only to come to a dead stop when I did. The change before me was not anything I'd set about doing myself. Between the two of us, we had money to last for generations to come, but I never went crazy spending. I'd long dreamed of having an amazing closet but was never able to justify the change in my head, particularly since what had been there previously had been absolutely fine, with tons of custom built-in storage and hanging space. It always just felt bland and utilitarian to me.

The closet he'd replaced it with was completely the opposite. I felt like Carrie Bradshaw in the *Sex and the City* movie. My eyes were wide as I took in the changes. The gold pendant lights were now a thing of the past, replaced by recessed lights and a beautiful chandelier. There were drawers on both sides, a massive island in the middle of the space and a small sitting area at the back of the room with two overstuffed chairs and an ottoman. The highlight of the renovation was the wall of floor to ceiling shoe storage on my side of the closet. It was so beautiful I almost squealed.

More unbelievable than all of the space was that it was full. I'd been sure he'd have had my New York stuff packed away after I left, but he hadn't. As I ran my hand along a row of blouses, I recognized some things that had come from my apartment in Jersey. I stopped moving, my lips pursed together as I stared at them. It wasn't that I'd thought for a second that he might be bluffing about all my things being packed up, but this was a step too far. He'd had my things moved without consulting me at all. The awe of the closet faded away as I gritted my teeth. He really was too damn high-handed sometimes. I was half inclined to storm into his office and have it out with him, but I knew that wasn't the answer.

A wave of anxiety hit me hard when I fully realized someone had packed my things. It meant their packing would have included the jeans at the top of my closet—the very pair that held my engagement ring.

I walked to the wall of drawers on my side of the closet and began opening them one by one until I found the first drawer of jeans. I pawed through it frantically, my heart rate accelerating when I didn't find the jeans. Ripping open the next drawer, I breathed a sigh of relief when I found the correct pair right on top, the velvet box still tucked safely away in the pocket. I pulled it out and flipped the lid open to be sure the ring was still there. It sparkled invitingly against the velvet lining of the box, silently calling for me to put it on.

It was though I was in some kind of a trance as I pulled it out and dropped the box into the drawer without care. I held the ring between my thumb and index finger, turning it side to side as I stared at it before sliding it into place. It was like I couldn't help it. What was worse was that it wasn't the first, second, or even the tenth time I'd put it on since I'd called off the engagement. Every night I'd been in Jersey City I'd found myself in my closet slipping it onto my ring finger. I'd lost too much weight for it to fit the way it was supposed to, which bothered me to no end. So much so that I'd gone as far as to order a ring sizer from Amazon. I stared down at my hand for several minutes before forcing myself to take it off and return it to the box, which I then slipped back into the jeans before shutting the drawer.

Desperate for a distraction from my thoughts, I

continued going through the drawers until I found the one full of swimsuits. I grabbed the one right on top, a simple pale yellow string bikini. In the drawer below it I found all of my bathing suit cover-ups, I pulled out a black and gold tunic before heading to my dressing room and vanity area that was just off the closet. I wasn't even surprised when I opened the door and realized the finishes matched the closet, right down to the smaller chandelier that hung above me. The vanity was a custom piece that was done in the same wood as the closet. I sighed as I shut the door behind me and stepped into the room, trying not to twirl like a little girl. Damn him. He knew me too well.

I sat down at the vanity, nodding my head as I surveyed how perfectly done the storage that surrounded it was. I spent a few minutes figuring out where everything went before I took off my earrings and put my hair up so it wouldn't get wet in the pool. A frustrated sound escaped me as I got into my bathing suit and saw the way it hung on me. The only thing saving the situation was that it was a string bikini, which meant I was able to tighten everything so it would stay on.

In the weeks after the accident, I'd lost seventeen pounds. Mateo had been beside himself, as had my doctor, but I'd felt nothing when food was put in front of me. Since leaving Spain I'd managed to put on four pounds, but I was still a shell of my former self and it frustrated me. I figured being bothered was a good thing since for so long I hadn't been able to drum up any concern for my own health.

I pushed all thoughts of the last year from my mind

as I grabbed a towel and made my way back into the bedroom. I then picked up my purse and pulled out my sunglasses, phone, and ear buds before opening the door to the hallway. The coast was clear, so I closed the door behind me quietly before scurrying toward the living room and out to the terrace.

The outdoor space was enormous and had always been my favorite hideaway when we were in New York. Immediately outside the sliders from the living room there were two tables that each had six chairs around them. To the left of that area was the outdoor kitchen and grill. Along the back of the terrace there were a few seating areas arranged around large potted trees. All of that was wonderful, but it was the pool that took up the right hand side of the area that I'd always gravitated to. I walked over and set my towel, phone and ear buds down on a chaise lounge before pulling my cover up over my head and laying it over the back of the cushion.

I headed for the small outbuilding in the corner of the terrace. It had a bathroom, a changing area, refrigerated drinks, snacks and a small bar. After punching in the code for the door, I entered and took a bottle of water. I quickly perused the magazine basket, choosing the most recent *Vanity Fair* as my reading material. I then stopped at the closet and pulled out a raft before exiting back to the pool area. I dropped the raft into the pool, set down my magazine and water and then headed directly into the pool. I knew without checking the temperature it would be a perfect eighty-seven degrees. The warm water embraced me as I waded in, just as I'd known it would. I floated through the water for about half an hour before settling onto the raft and closing my eyes.

I'd been doing my best to avoid it all, to put it out of my mind, but it wasn't possible. I'd gone from my tiny office to the home I'd vowed never to see again within the space of a few hours and the fiancé I'd bailed on was insisting that the wedding was back on. I was overwhelmed and confused, unsure of how to proceed. I'd been so sure Mateo would've moved on once I left, but he seemed more determined than ever that we marry.

The idea of spending a lifetime with someone who spoke about me the way he had wasn't okay. On the other hand, neither was dealing with dividing up Cruz Saez Holdings. Mateo wasn't wrong when he said thousands of people would lose their jobs. I'd offered to sell my half to Antonio after I postponed the wedding, but he wasn't having any part of it.

*"Half this business belongs to you and as long as I am alive, it always will," he'd told me. "Quino would never forgive me if you walked away from this, no matter how much money you made from the sale. We built this life together for each other as the brothers we always believed we should have been, which makes this a family business. The intent was always to pass that on to our children. Without you, half of the family would be gone and my brother's dream would go along with it. I promised him I would step in to be here for you when he no longer could be. I will not break that vow."*

The mention of my father had cracked my weak resolve and I'd dropped the subject, promising Antonio everything would work out. I'd lied to him, and to Camila when I told them I just needed time to find myself and heal. Back then, all I'd been able to focus on was getting away because I'd been too exhausted and broken down to deal with anything else.

A little less than two hours after I'd come outside, I heard Mateo clearing his throat from the pool deck. I turned his way with a scowl, annoyed that he couldn't leave me alone.

He paid no attention to my air of hostility. This was because his eyes were busy looking me over lasciviously. My internal temperature began to climb the longer it went on, and that just wouldn't do.

"What do you want?"

He didn't look even a little bit repentant when he brought his eyes up to my face.

"You are not ready for what I want. For now, I have lunch," he said, gesturing to one of the outdoor tables.

I was in no mood to break bread with him, so I didn't bother looking to see what he'd brought.

"I'm not hungry," I said as I turned my nose up disdainfully.

"You will come out of the pool and eat or I will come in and get you. It is past time to get back to normal, Ava."

The raft I was on rocked unsteadily as I turned and glared at him. "Don't you dare try to boss me around like you're my father!"

He had the good grace to look chastised.

"I did not mean—"

"What I eat and when is not your business!"

"It is my business, more than anyone else's. I would expect you to do the same for me if I had wasted away in front of your eyes."

I swallowed hard, looking away guiltily. "I've gained some weight back," I said quietly.

His sigh traveled over me like a caress.

"If you did, it was a pound or two, maybe."

"Actually, it's four," I corrected.

"That is a drop in the bucket and you know it. Stop pushing me away and let me help," he demanded. "You need to eat, Ava. I had security run to Junior's Restaurant for your favorites. There is a grilled Reuben with extra sauerkraut and a slice of cheesecake for dessert right here waiting for you."

My mouth watered the second he mentioned the sandwich. I'd been so cut off in Jersey that I hadn't really left my apartment much. My daily schedule had been lather, rinse and repeat. Get up, have a yogurt, take an Uber to work, do boring data entry for hours on end, take an Uber home and end my day with a can of soup and a piece of French bread. On Mondays I had a standing appointment with my therapist and for the last five weeks on Thursdays I went to a trauma survivors support group. That carefully regimented scheduled had been the sum total of my social activity. Even my groceries had been delivered.

The one and only time I'd gone out socially had been the previous night. Our group leader had assigned us to pair up and have dinner in a restaurant. We'd pulled names from a hat, and I'd gotten Eric, who I had been out with the night before. Eric was happily married with three children, just trying to find his way back to normalcy after he was held hostage for five hours during a bank robbery gone very wrong.

Eric and I were friendly but not at all close. The dinner had been okay, albeit a bit uncomfortable since both of us weren't used to social situations anymore. I'd barely eaten during the meal because I'd been overwhelmed by how loud the restaurant was. He'd talked a lot about his wife—she'd chosen the restaurant we went to—while I'd kept it boring with work stories. The reason I'd been in Jersey City to begin with was that it was off the grid. Offering up detail about myself would've been counter-productive.

"Avelina," Mateo growled, pulling me from my thoughts. "Please get out of the pool and eat."

Part of me was tempted to flip him off, but a larger part wanted some of the damn Reuben. I mumbled expletives under my breath as I pushed myself up and over the side of the raft. Swimming to the steps, I huffed out a sound when I saw him standing at the entrance to the pool holding a towel for me. I needed space and he wasn't giving me any. Stepping out of the pool, I yanked the towel from his hand and wrapped it around myself. I then headed directly to the table the food was on and chose a seat. I should've been prepared for him to sit right next to me, but I wasn't. When he pulled the chair out, sat down and angled himself toward me, my pulse started racing.

"There are six other chairs," I choked out. "Why can't you sit in one of them?"

"Have we ever sat apart?"

I shook my head. "No, but—"

"But nothing. This is our reality. We sit close, we touch often and we can not keep our hands off each other. It is not a crime."

My mouth went so dry it felt like a small desert town.

"I can't eat with you so close," I croaked.

His eyes squeezed closed as he took a deep breath. When he opened them, he reached onto my plate, picked up half of the Reuben and brought it to my mouth.

"I am not moving. You will eat."

I stiffened and moved my head back. "I'm able to feed myself," I answered.

"And yet you do not," he said gently. "I have been patient to the point of physical pain. I have acceded to your wishes and given you the space you begged for. All of the decisions I made to keep you happy and free of stress did not improve this situation. You buried yourself under a mountain of fear and anxiety, refusing any help. It has not worked, mi bello amor. Now, we play by my rules."

My eyes widened. "Rules?"

"Sí."

I gulped as I stared at him dumbly, unable to form a response.

"Abre tu boca, Ava."

His telling me to open my mouth was a clear indicator he wasn't going to back down. I'm not sure exactly why, but I followed his command and took a bite of the sandwich, trying not to look at him as I did so. The rich and savory flavor of the Reuben spread across my tongue, the taste so good I couldn't hold back a little mmmm sound.

He waved me off when I went to take the sandwich from me so I could continue eating, instead holding the food up to my lips again for me to take another bite.

"Why are you doing this?"

His eyes held mine as he reached out with his free

hand to trace a finger down the bridge of my nose.

"It is my privilege to take care of you," he answered. "Do not fight me on this."

There were so many things I could've said, but I couldn't force any past my lips. Instead, I took the path of least resistance and nodded my consent. When he lifted the sandwich, I took another bite. It went on that way until I'd finished. When he reached onto my plate to pick up the other half, I stopped him. Although it was delicious and my mouth absolutely wanted more, my stomach was over full.

"I can't eat any more right now. I'm stuffed."

His brow furrowed, as he looked me over. "It was not enough food," he grumbled.

"Cut me some slack," I huffed. "That thing was huge. Eating half was an achievement. I'll wrap the other half up and eat it later, along with some of the cheesecake."

He nodded as he leaned back in his seat and ran his hands through his hair. "I guess they do make a big sandwich," he conceded.

Being so close to him was addling my brain. Anxious to get some distance, I pushed myself back from the table and stood.

"I need to go change."

He said nothing as he walked to the sliding glass door where he stood and waited for me while I picked up the magazine and water I'd left on the lounger. I could feel his eyes raking over me as I walked across the patio. I bit my lip and kept my eyes focused on anything other than him as I brushed past him on my way back inside. Just that simple bit of contact had my pulse skyrocketing and I'd had to beat back the urge to seek the comfort of his arms. I'd never felt more secure or at peace than I did when he held me. No matter how hard I tried I couldn't seem to change my natural reaction to him.

I scurried down the hall to the bedroom and closed the door behind me, letting out a relieved breath as I leaned my back against it. In a matter of just a few hours, Mateo had broken through my defenses. I slid down to the floor, bending my knees so I could wrap my arms around my legs and pull them close to my chest.

The thing that scared me the most was that he wanted me to remember. I knew Mateo, which meant I knew he wouldn't give up until everything was out in the open.

We were never going to agree on that when I was one hundred percent sure I needed to keep those memories buried deep.

# Seven

*Ava—Three years ago*

"IS THIS WHAT YOU WORE TO GRADUATION?"

Shock rippled through me as I finished washing my hands. I held in a grimace as I turned off the faucet and dried my hands on a towel before turning around. As usual, she was perfectly coiffed from head to toe. Her blonde hair was swept up into a neat-as-a-pin chignon and her navy blue ensemble all but screamed couture. With the addition of her jewelry—she only ever wore obscenely large diamonds and pearls—and the sky-high pair of Louboutin's on her feet, my mother was easily wearing the equivalent of the down payment on a house.

I ignored her question, instead voicing one of my own. "You were due here yesterday and you haven't answered any of my calls. Where have you been?"

She rolled her eyes as though my question was silly. "I was in Paris for almost three weeks," she answered.

It had been almost a full year since I'd last seen her and she didn't speak to me much, either. Still, I'd expected her to show some interest in my graduation. As usual, I was disappointed.

"You got back from Paris last week," I pointed out stiffly. I knew this not because she kept in touch, but because she'd posted photos on her Instagram.

"Obviously you know nothing about unpacking after a shopping trip. It takes days, if not weeks to organize a couture closet after a major shopping trip."

I crossed my arms over my chest and narrowed my eyes at her.

"And somehow that kept you from answering your phone?"

She looked over my shoulder at the mirror and ran her hand over her hair, making sure it was smooth. My normal reaction to her behavior would have been to fill the silence, but I was over that. It dragged out uncomfortably before she finally responded.

"Busy is busy, Lina. My social calendar is always very full."

Her social calendar? I was her *daughter*. Our relationship had always been unconventional, but she was stooping to a new low.

"One would think your only child graduating from high school would've rated higher in your calendar," I said stiffly.

The expression on her face was blank.

"I'm here now. That should be good enough for you."

Even though it wasn't unusual for her to behave the way she was, it still rankled. The saving grace for me was that it hurt less than it used to.

It dawned on me then that she had just walked into

the bathroom of the restaurant we'd chosen to celebrate Dio, Rafe and my graduation as if she owned the place. I assumed she'd spoken to my father, but that made me wonder why he hadn't told me she really was going to make it.

"Why didn't you reach out to tell me you were going to be late? You took the time to contact Papá to tell him you were coming, why not me?"

"I most certainly did not. That perfectly wretched long-lost Cruz kid was on the jet with me from New York. When we landed, his driver brought us here."

He had come! My eyes had widened for a fraction of a second before I remembered to school my expression. I was no fool. If my mother knew I was interested in Mateo, she would lose her marbles. The only person she hated as much as my father was Antonio. The entire Cruz family was persona non grata to her.

Beneath my carefully guarded exterior, I was suddenly a bundle of nerves. He had been scheduled to arrive this morning. When he hadn't shown up and didn't contact me, I'd feared he was blowing the event off entirely. I hadn't expected that from him at all, and it hurt like hell. More so than my mother's absence, Mateo's cut deep.

Although he was living in New York City full-time while working, Mateo and I grew closer by the day. During the first month or so our conversations had been all about my father and his healing process. Bit by bit that gave way to talking about more and more things until a real friendship was established. Now we emailed, texted, talked or Skyped daily. I hadn't heard from him all day, which was upsetting to me. Knowing he'd come, relaxed something inside of me.

My mother broke my train of thought when she cleared her throat to get my attention.

"Would it have killed you to choose nice shoes? It's like you were trying to look foolish."

Of course she was going there. I wouldn't have expected otherwise.

"I'm quite happy with my outfit."

She wrinkled her nose as she scrutinized my outfit. "I don't know why," she said disdainfully. "I can tell that not one thing you're wearing comes from an appropriate designer."

My eyes were dying to roll, but somehow I kept it in. I loved my white bodycon mini dress with its lace sleeves and back. I felt good about the way I looked, but I wasn't surprised my mother didn't care for it. All told the outfit had cost less than two hundred dollars. To my mother, that was as offensive as farting in public.

I shrugged, brushing her critique off. Tía Camila had cried and told me how beautiful I looked at least a half dozen times while she took photos of me with Rafe and Dio before and after the graduation ceremony.

Only now did I fully understand that ten months without my mother around hadn't been a bad thing as far as my self-confidence went.

"As lovely as this is, I'm not going to stand in the bathroom with you all day, Mother. I'll see you when you come out."

She huffed out an annoyed sound as I stalked out without a backward glance. The instant the door closed behind me, I sprinted back to the private dining room the small family dinner for our graduation was in.

My eyes went directly to Mateo, who was standing talking to his father and mine. He seemed agitated, his hand waving in a gesture of annoyance as he spoke. Even from across the room I was able to tell he was speaking in rapid-fire Spanish.

Quite abruptly he stopped talking, his head turning toward the doorway I was standing in. He smiled at the same time I did, almost as if we'd choreographed it. He gestured toward me with his hand as he said something to our fathers before breaking away from them and coming straight to me.

I walked toward him with purpose only to slow down when it hit me that I wasn't sure how to greet him. I wanted to hug him but was unsure if I should. He'd hugged me frequently at Thanksgiving, Christmas, and Easter when he'd been in Spain but I had never initiated one before. Were we at the point where we hugged all the time? I thought so but since I wasn't positive, it made me timid.

The question was answered when he wrapped his arms around me, enveloping me in a warm embrace as he lifted me up and spun me in a circle.

"I missed you so much," he murmured. "You have no idea how long I have waited for this."

I couldn't help the way I melted against him, nor was I able to contain the happy sigh that escaped me. I allowed myself to enjoy the feel of his chest beneath my cheek to the count of five, and then I looked up into the green eyes that made me weak in the knees.

"I missed you just as much. I'm so glad you're here!" I squeaked as I took a step back.

He let me go but stepped forward so that we were still close.

"You look so beautiful."

I felt my cheeks heat up as I bit my lip and glanced away, trying to hold in my grin. Mateo had said I was beautiful.

"Thank you," I answered shyly as I looked back up and met his gaze.

The intensity of the way he stared at me made my stomach feel like I'd just swallowed a box of baking soda and chased it with a glass of vinegar.

"I was scared you weren't going to come at all," I blurted.

I immediately regretted my loose lips when a look of anger flashed across Mateo's face. Before I could question it, his expression changed back to normal.

"I am unhappy to have let you down. If it had been up to me, I would have been here before the graduation ceremony. Something came up that had to be dealt with, but I would not miss your celebration for the world," he explained. "Come hell or high water; I was getting myself here today."

I assumed whatever it was likely related to his job. "Is everything okay?"

He nodded. "Everything is perfect now that I am here with you, where I belong."

I could tell whatever it was he had to take care of had annoyed him. For a few moments, I allowed myself to fantasize about how great it would be if he quit his job in America and moved back to Spain. If he did, we'd be able to see each other all of the time.

"How long can you stay?"

He smiled as though he knew I was anxious to spend time with him.

"Seven days," he answered. "And I will spend every single one of them with you. I plan to monopolize your time horribly."

I grinned like a fool because that was exactly what I wanted.

"Well, well, well. I should've known that caveman act wasn't just because of her father," my mother said acidly as she stepped from behind Mateo.

His jaw ticked as his eyes flared, clearly annoyed by the interruption. I wasn't thrilled about it, either. He turned to face her but positioned himself right by my side, almost like he was protecting me from her.

"There's no need to be rude, Mother," I reprimanded. "It's a celebration. Please don't create a scene."

One of her perfectly arched eyebrows went up as she pursed her lips and shrugged me off.

"I get to be as rude as I want to be since I was man-handled by this brute today."

Mateo went so stiff I thought he might turn to stone.

"I did not touch you," he snapped.

"Perhaps not, but you know you bullied me," she countered.

"What are you talking about?" I asked.

"I'm talking about this… this person waiting for me in the lobby of my building when I came home at one in the morning! He was rude and completely out of bounds, insisting I come with him to Spain. I said no, but he wouldn't give up until I agreed. He practically dragged me to the plane, Lina! It was demeaning and completely un-called for."

My breath caught in my throat as the implications of her rant hit me. Mateo had been late because he'd been busy making sure my mother would be here. I was more touched than I could say by his actions, but very angry with my mother.

"Are you telling me the only reason you're here right now is because Mateo forced you to come?" I asked, my voice deceptively soft.

Mateo shifted uncomfortably at my side, his hand rubbing at my back soothingly. "Avelina—"

I held up my hand to him. "Stop. I asked my mother a question. She needs to answer it."

She didn't look even a little bit chastised.

"I told you I was busy," she reminded me. "I don't ap-preciate being bullied. Need I remind you that it was you who chose this life, Lina?"

Her words were a verbal slap to the face.

"Are you really going to continue to hold a grudge be-cause I wanted to stay here after my father almost died?" I asked incredulously.

"What's going on over here?" Papá asked.

My eyes widened when I realized he and Tío Antonio had made their way over to us. The expression on his face made me anxious. Not that he'd hurt her—I knew he would never raise a hand to a woman—but because I was scared the stress of any confrontation would cause him another heart attack. I worried about him obsessively and seeing him get worked up about anything scared the hell out of me.

"Everything is fine," I assured him.

He reached out and squeezed my hand in his. I held on tight as he turned and faced my mother.

"Karen," he said cordially. "How nice that you are here. It is quite an amazing thing to have our child graduate high school, yes?"

"Sure, Joaquin," she answered in a bored sounding voice, "it's just peachy. A living reminder that I'm getting older is such a pleasure and being dragged from my home in order to be here was the cherry on top of my day."

My shoulders slumped in defeat. It couldn't be more obvious that she was only here under duress. I found her behavior embarrassing and disheartening all at the same time. I thought perhaps Dio was right—he'd long said I should cut her off. Not only had nothing changed, she was worse than ever.

"You should leave. Now."

I'd spoken loud enough that the room went silent. My mother's jaw dropped for a fraction of a second before she recovered her composure.

"Watch how you talk to me, little girl," she said coldly. "I could so easily rock your little world."

"Don't threaten my daughter," my father responded, completely ignoring my mother's rude scoff. Turning back to me he continued, "It will be fine, mi ángel. Do not stress yourself. Karen just needs a drink and a few minutes to unwind from the long journey."

I loved him for trying, but enough was enough.

"No. She needs to leave. She's told me multiple times in the mere minutes she's been here that she doesn't want to be. I'm over it. Go back to New York, Mother. Finish unpacking your new wardrobe."

"Don't think I won't walk right out of here without looking back," she huffed, like it was some kind of a threat.

"I'm telling you to do just that," I shrugged. "Today isn't about you. It's about me, Rafe and Dio. You need to go."

Her back went ramrod straight as she narrowed her eyes and glared at me. "You're just like him," she sneered.

"You say that as if it's an insult when nothing could be farther from the truth. I love my father and I am proud to be like him."

"It damn well figures you'd say that," she huffed, "since you've always been a spoiled little brat."

When my father stepped forward angrily, I whimpered. I couldn't help my natural fear that anger would lead to another heart attack.

"That is enough," Antonio snapped, taking control of the situation so my father didn't have to. "Your daughter has told you to leave and since she's the only reason we were going to tolerate your presence, that leaves you unwelcome."

He inclined his head toward Mateo before continuing. "My son will instruct security to drive you back to the airport while I alert the pilot to prepare a return flight to New York. Have a nice flight."

She shrugged it off like it was nothing. "Thanks for forcing me to waste an entire day on this nonsense," she said before turning and stalking from the room without another word to me.

Mateo spoke from my side. "I will be right back. Stay with your father."

Antonio kissed my forehead before pulling his phone from his pocket and leaving the room to make travel arrangements. Papá wrapped his arms around me and pulled me in against his chest.

"I am sorry, mi ángel. I would not have asked Mateo to stop at nothing to get her here if I'd known she would behave the way she just did."

When he loosened his hold on me, I reached up and kissed his cheek. "Don't worry about me," I said calmly. "She's been ridiculous for the last ten months and to-night was the straw that broke the camel's back. It doesn't change how wonderful this day has been. Maybe another day I'll be upset, but for tonight, I just want to forget her entirely."

The graduation after party at the Cruz's was official-ly winding down. It was a smallish gathering of fami-ly, friends from school and a few of the employees from Cruz Saez that Rafe, Dio and I had known for years.

After my mother had departed the restaurant, I no-ticed everyone was darn near breaking their necks to monitor me, like I was a delicate flower about to droop. Was I happy that my mother had been so cold? Not at all, but it didn't mean I was going to fall apart. I'd told her to leave because she needed to. I figured I'd deal with what-ever the aftermath was later. After almost losing my fa-ther, I had learned to prioritize.

Mateo stayed by my side for the majority of the evening, which was my favorite part of the whole day. Currently, he was huddled with his dad and his brothers, but I felt confident he'd return to me when he was finished talking.

Officially eighteen and now a high school graduate, I had high hopes that perhaps my feelings were reciprocated. I had near constant butterflies in my stomach whenever he looked at me, and the sound of his voice melted me like butter. My senses told me something big was coming, but I was afraid to count on it. If I did and nothing happened, it would break my heart.

We had gotten so close over the previous ten months it meant there wasn't much we didn't discuss. Barcelona was six hours ahead of New York, so he called me each day on his lunch break, which was at one o'clock his time.

*"Tell me about your day,"* he said.

*"Boring,"* I answered as I spun around in the chair in front of the desk in my room. *"I went to school, came home and did some homework with Dio, ate dinner with my father and then waited for you to call. Tell me about yours."*

*"Long and frustrating,"* he sighed. *"I sat through two extremely tedious meetings this morning. After that, I spent an hour with a web developer learning about coupon codes. I watched the clock the whole time, praying time would move faster so I could talk to you sooner. I hate not being in Spain."*

*"It will be over before you know it,"* I lied.

*Each day felt like an eternity, but I couldn't tell him that.*

*"Too long,"* he groaned. *"The days drag terribly."*

*"You should go out with your friends and try to have fun."*

*He made a dismissive sound. "Their idea of fun is to*

*troll bars looking for women, something I have no interest in. I am happy to play basketball with them on Saturday afternoons, but that is about it. Things will get better when summer comes and I am able to spend some time at home with you."*

All signs pointed to him liking me, but until he flat out said it, I was afraid to count on it. I loved that he wasn't out raising the roof and bringing wild women back to his apartment. The amount of time he spent talking to or emailing me let me know he wasn't a swinging bachelor. Lord knows he could have been.

I'd gone through his Facebook feed like a wannabe private investigator and hadn't found anything current I felt I should worry about. I went back to the start of all the photos he had posted, and the last girlfriend I found was from the first year of college. Her name was Jill, and they dated for three or four months. I vaguely recalled Antonio, Camila, and my father talking about having lunch with her once, but back then I hadn't been interested in Mateo, which meant I hadn't paid close attention.

Aesthetically, Jill was the complete opposite of me. I'm a brunette and she's a redhead. I'm on the shorter side of the spectrum while she's super tall. I'm so-so about school, while her Facebook page says she's a molecular biologist. I'd be lying if I said that didn't bother me. If super smart collegiate women are Mateo's preference, I was going to be out of luck. I'm not a dolt, but I couldn't do molecular biology for any amount of money.

Anxious to take my mind off of what may or may not ever happen with Mateo and me, I started rolling one of the bar carts back to the pool house. Now that we were adults and all of our friends are eighteen, drinking was allowed. It was funny how once it became legal we all seemed to care less. Both of the bar carts were loaded with unopened liquor bottles, and the keg on the patio was still half full.

Humming softly, I rolled the cart into the back of the room next to the built in bar. The next morning the cleaning staff would organize everything, so I didn't need to do anything else. Spinning on my heel to leave, I came to a halt when I saw Mateo leaning against the sliding glass door jam watching me.

My hand went to my throat as I let out a soft gasp. "You scared me," I squeaked. "I swear you're half X-Man or something. I never hear you approaching."

He let out a husky sounding chuckle as he crossed the room to me. "In the future, I will attempt to make as much noise as a herd of elephants."

I swallowed nervously as he approached me. The way he was looking at me was new, and it had me reeling. My skin felt tighter, and my heartbeat seemed louder. Even looking at him felt different. Everything was somehow more.

My breathing stalled for a moment when he stopped in front of me, too close for there to be any misunderstanding of his intention. The feel of his body heat whetted my appetite exponentially. I'd never felt anything like it, but some part of me knew what I was experiencing was more than lust. When I remembered to take another breath, the heady scent of him engulfed my senses.

He lifted his right hand and set it against my neck, just over my pulse point.

"You are officially an adult now," he said, his voice rich and seductive.

My eyes felt heavy-lidded as I nodded.

"Are you ready for this?" he asked.

I didn't have to ask what he meant. I knew exactly. My senses had been right all along—Mateo Cruz wanted me. I licked my lips and nodded as I reached up and set my hands on his shoulders.

"Be sure," he growled. "Once you are mine, there will be no way back. This is not transitory."

God, I hoped not. The way I felt about Mateo wasn't anything that would dissipate over time.

"Yours?" I asked breathlessly.

"Mine," he confirmed.

I nodded again.

"Say it," he commanded.

"Yes, Mateo."

"Yes, what?"

I was so lost in the emerald swirl of his eyes; I didn't answer immediately. Instead, I leaned into him, a shiver running up my spine as I felt the warmth of his chest through my dress.

"Avelina," he prompted gently. "I will not touch you unless you say the words I need to hear."

"I'm yours, Mateo," I whispered.

He growled out something fast and low in Spanish, words I didn't quite catch. Before I could ask him to repeat himself, his lips were against mine. At that point, I forgot any and all questions I'd ever had about anything because his tongue was gliding across my lower lip. The hand at my neck held me in place as he deepened the kiss.

When he touched his tongue to mine for the first time, something inside of me shifted as a piece of my puzzle found it's home.

I gripped his shoulders and held on tight as we kissed. I moaned when his free hand slid down to my waist, pulling me in closer, the only thing between us being the clothing we were wearing.

I'd never known kissing could feel that way. It was carnal and heated while somehow being tender at the same time. I felt like a live wire as different sensations assaulted my system, each one leaving me wanting more.

"Como el cielo," he growled as he broke away and began raining soft kisses along my jawline.

He was right; it was heaven. I nodded my agreement as my breath came in frantic gusts.

I shivered and moaned as he traced his tongue along the outer shell of my ear.

"Mateo," I moaned.

He kissed me again. Gone was the sweet reserve. In its place was a thorough claiming that had me rubbing against him as though I was in heat. He pulled away after countless minutes, his breathing just as labored as mine.

"I knew we would be fire," he said as he set his forehead against mine.

I blinked up at him in confusion. "Why did you stop?"

"Because we are just lucky not to have been interrupted."

I frowned uneasily. Were we going to try to keep the change in our relationship a secret? That didn't make me feel very good at all.

"Are we hiding this from everyone?" I asked.

He placed both hands behind my neck, running his fingers up and down below my hairline.

"Absolutely not," he declared firmly. "I already told Quino and my father that this was coming. I did not want there to be any problem."

My mouth dropped open for a half a second before I snapped it shut.

"You did?"

"Of course I did," he rasped. "I would never do anything that could hurt you. I needed to make sure everyone was on board from the get-go. "

"Papá was okay with it?"

"More than okay," Mateo chuckled. "He has known for quite a while, Ava. He gave me his blessing at Easter."

"I'm glad to hear it," I laughed.

"There is nothing in our way," he said softly. "Everyone knows and is happy about it. We could not ask for better support."

I parted my lips to respond but snapped them shut when the pool house door flew open. I sprang away from Mateo in time to see Alejandro wheeling in the other bar cart. Rather than stay separated, Mateo wrapped his arms around my waist and pulled my back against his front.

"I see you two are really a thing now?" he asked teasingly.

"We are everything," Mateo confirmed.

I just beamed like a fool because I'd never been happier.

Mateo Cruz was mine.

# Eight

*Ava—Present*

I WAS TOO KEYED UP AND ANXIOUS TO LOSE MYSELF IN anything. After showering and drying my hair, I tried to read a book on my iPad. I gave up after about twenty-minutes of reading the same page. Next, I moved to the bedroom sitting area and tried to settle in to watch something. After what felt like the thousandth time of going through the channel guide, I turned it off. I was too amped up, which meant it wasn't going to happen.

The only thing I knew would pass the time would be to make food. I loved to cook but hadn't done it in forever. With my mind made up, I made my way into the kitchen. It was a cook's dream, full of restaurant-grade appliances that made cooking pure joy. My first stop was the refrigerator, which quickly pulled me up short when I opened it. Mateo always kept it stocked, so I'd been confident I'd have no problem finding something to whip up. The fridge I'd assumed would be full was almost completely barren. Instead of the well-organized shelves I'd been expecting, I only found the leftovers from what he'd fed me earlier. The rest of the contents were condiments.

"Sorry," he said from behind me. "I meant to have my assistant go to the store, but the day got away from me. I will make sure it is done first thing in the morning."

I spun around to face him suspiciously. "You said you'd been in New York this whole time, but the fridge looks exactly the way it does when we come in from Spain. Were you staying somewhere else?"

"Yes," he answered, without offering any additional information.

"Here in New York?" I pressed.

He turned away to open one of the beverage drawers at the island and pulled out a bottle of water.

"More or less," he mumbled as he twisted the lid off and took a sip.

My stomach churned as I glared at him. He *had* been out getting his kicks.

"I'm not stupid," I spat angrily. "You were living the bachelor life. You don't need to hide it from me you jerk! Just admit that you were out there screwing—"

"That is enough!" he snapped as he set the bottle down on the counter. "Your allegations are baseless. I have not touched another woman in more than four years. Even in the seconds before you turned around that night, I knew that was it for me. My soul sent me a message I heard loud and clear, one I did not and could not misinterpret. No one has or will tempt me to stray from the person I want. I will touch you and only you, forever."

Damn my stupid heart for melting the way it did.

"If that's true, you shouldn't have any issue telling me

where you've been staying, but you're being weird about it," I challenged.

He ran his hand along the back of his neck as he looked at me bashfully.

"You really need to know where I was?"

"Either tell me or don't," I retorted. "You being secretive is telling a tale of its own."

He barked out a harsh laugh. "Oh, Ava… that tale is probably *far* less pathetic than the truth."

I stayed silent but continued glaring daggers at him.

He sighed heavily and rubbed at his temples. "I followed after you and rented an apartment in the building across the street from yours in Jersey City. Do you feel better now that you know?"

My jaw went slack as I gaped at him. I'd been so sure he'd let me leave because he wanted his freedom. Following me out to Jersey didn't align with that at all.

"Why?"

The look he gave me was one of pure frustration. "Because I love you so much that I can not live without you," he answered. "Which, if you were thinking straight, you would have known without asking."

It was like a sucker punch to the gut. Did he really think I'd believe that after what I'd heard?

"How can you say that with a straight face?" I asked angrily.

His look was a mixture of disbelief and frustration. "Because it is true!" he bellowed. "I wake up thinking about you. I fall asleep thinking about you. And when I dream, I dream about *you* because you are my *life*, Ava. How many more ways can I show you that before you remember it is a fact? You once were more certain of my love than anything else. Why have you allowed yourself to forget this? No matter what lies you were told or what we lost in the process, you should have known better!"

I sucked in a harsh breath as the emotion on his face sliced at my heart with surgical precision. I felt oddly defensive, like I was the one at fault.

"You say that like I didn't have evidence—"

"Do *not* call that carefully edited and manipulated bullshit evidence. It was as fake as the person who gave it to you."

"Of course you get to say that because there's no way to prove otherwise. I heard what I heard, Mateo. Do you imagine I wanted my life to be ripped apart? I could have died!"

He visibly blanched, his eyes full of pain. "You say that as if I would *ever* forget," he said hoarsely. "Never have I known such terror, Ava. Had you gone, I would have been lost to this life as well."

His obvious angst destroyed me, enough so that I felt it necessary to reassure him in some way.

"I survived," I reminded him. "I'm still here. *I'm fine.*"

His shoulders sagged as he looked away. "I would hardly say you are fine when you have never been farther away."

I opened my lips to respond, but no words came.

"I just… I cannot do this," he said tiredly before he turned and left the kitchen.

A minute later I heard the sound of the elevator doors opening. I hurried to the living room, arriving just in time to see the doors closing with him inside.

We made eye contact for a second, and in that time I saw something in his eyes that almost brought me to my knees.

Mateo was frustrated and hurt—and both of those emotions were directed at me.

# Nine

*Ava—Three years ago*

THE ONLY DOWNSIDE TO BEING MATEO'S girlfriend was the physical distance of my living in Spain while he was in New York. He'd committed to working for the American grocery chain at the entry level for two years, which kept him from moving back to Barcelona after college. With one year down, he still had another to go.

He hated that he'd opted to do it—but at the time he and I hadn't been together, nor had we known we would be. When destiny set us on the path we were on together, he'd already had the job. It meant he couldn't come to Barcelona on a whim, which sucked. To that end, I was on a jet to New York to spend the next four weeks with him before I had to be back for the start of the fall semester.

It had been wonderful having him in Spain for the week following my graduation, but an entire month had passed since then. Like an idiot I'd signed up for three summer classes at the University, never realizing Mateo and I would officially be a couple by then. I'd been anxious to get my degree underway, but in retrospect, I wished I had waited.

When I got off the plane and saw Mateo waiting for me in the private terminal, I felt all lit up inside. I ran to him at top speed, smiling when I saw he was running too. I was so anxious to get to him that I dropped my purse as I jumped up into his arms.

"God, how I have missed you," he rasped just before his lips met mine.

I kissed him back passionately, unconcerned that there were other people in the terminal. I only cared about being in Mateo's arms. I moaned as our tongues performed a sensual dance. His hands cupped my face like a caress, as he tasted me, the skill of his kiss melting my brain more with each passing second. When he pulled back, I blinked up at him dazedly as he traced a thumb over my lower lip.

"Mine," he said hoarsely.

My eyes were heavy lidded as I darted my tongue out and licked the tip of his thumb.

"Yours," I confirmed.

He groaned low in his throat as he moved back the smallest fraction of an inch. "Do that again and you will get us arrested for public indecency. People are watching."

My cheeks heated as I turned my head to the right. Sure enough, a woman in the waiting area was perched on one of the leather seats watching us like we were a soap opera. I stifled a giggle as I stepped back from Mateo. I lost control when I was around him. He let out a laugh of his own as he bent down and retrieved my purse from the spot where I'd dropped it, handing it to me with a grin.

We were in our own little world as we left the airport. He walked with his arm around my shoulders and I leaned into him, loving how affectionate and demonstrative he was. He'd been the same way during his week in Spain after my graduation and I practically ate it up. He wasn't shy about staking his claim and making it clear to anyone with a pulse that we were a couple.

I was excited to see the penthouse he'd bought himself two months before. Prior to that, he'd been staying in an executive rental while searching for something he wanted to purchase. I'd been a little freaked out that he was buying a home in America, but he'd settled my fears with ease.

"This is a good long-term investment for our future. Because I know the American system so well now, my father has already decided that once I start at Cruz Saez, I will be in charge of overseeing the east coast operation. We will have to fly in every six to eight weeks or so for a few days."

"We?" I'd asked.

"Always we," he'd answered with no hesitation. "It is not just my apartment, Ava. It is ours."

That was Mateo's way. There was no hesitation, ever, in talking about the future. It was clear he saw us together, which made me ecstatic since I absolutely wanted the same thing. I fell deeper in love with him with every passing day.

He'd texted me a bunch of photos of the penthouse since he'd purchased it, but I was excited about seeing it in person. When we got into the elevator, he stood behind me and covered my eyes with his hands. "Are you ready to see your New York home?"

My smile was so wide I probably looked like The Joker as I leaned back into the firmness of his body. "I'm ready," I said enthusiastically.

When he pulled his hands away the first thing I saw was the amazing view. I oohed and aahed about it, completely in love with the beauty of Fifth Avenue that sprawled out forty stories below us. From up high you could appreciate the frenetic energy Manhattan had to offer while also enjoying the beauty of the sprawling landscape. The apartment had been custom decorated and offered fully furnished, so Mateo hadn't had to buy any furniture. I knew some people would say the décor was nice but I found it stiff and uninviting. Of course, I didn't say that to him. The view more than made up for the furniture.

Our shared joy in seeing each other again was quite evident. When we sat on the couch, Mateo pulled me onto his lap. It was like we couldn't be close enough. Over and over again mid-sentence one of us would lean in for a kiss and countless minutes would then pass while we lost ourselves in another soul-searing exchange of desire. Things were escalating quickly and I wasn't upset about it.

The feel of the thick length of his erection beneath me had me breathless with desire. Although we'd kissed hundreds of times during his week in Spain, being in New York completely alone together changed the experience. It was needy, carnal, and far more erotic than it had been before. I think it was because we knew there was no limit. We were completely free to explore each other without anyone interrupting. It was a heady experience to be sure.

I'd rearranged myself on his lap so that I was straddling him, the skirt of my gray and yellow dress yanked up high around my thighs as I rocked back and forth on him. His hands were wrapped in my hair as his tongue plundered my mouth, the taste of him more intoxicating than any alcohol. My hands were running up and down the solid wall of muscle beneath his shirt, desperate little moans erupting my throat as I kissed him back with abandon.

Mateo growled as he tugged at my hair and pulled me back. "Avelina," he rasped. "Too far, too fast."

"Don't stop," I begged. "Just a little bit more. It's so good to be with you like this."

His emerald eyes flashed like liquid fire as he stared at me. "Not yet. If we keep going, we will take it farther than we should."

I frowned down at him, a sliver of unease making its way up my spine.

"But you talk about us being together long term," I murmured. "Is that not real?"

"It is the most real, but we need to work our way up to more. You deserve better than a desperate pounding after a long flight. I am going to seduce you slowly," he said huskily.

My heart felt as though it might burst out of my chest. I'd believed that once you were in love, you stopped falling. I knew love would grow bigger and stronger over time, but not that you could find something new and different to fall more in love with all the time. With Mateo, I was learning just how wrong I was.

I cupped his face with both hands, tracing my thumbs over the thick stubble on his cheeks. Leaning in, I kissed him softly before pulling back and smiling down at him.

"You're incredible."

He leaned into my left hand and rubbed his cheek against my palm. "I have the most beautiful girl in the world in my arms telling me she thinks I am incredible. How lucky am I?"

"Pretty lucky," I said cheekily.

"The luckiest," he answered before pulling me in and kissing me reverently.

When it came time to go to bed that night, there wasn't even a question of where I would sleep. Truth be told, I was fairly certain that we wouldn't be able to be apart from each other for that length of time—not when we were in the same apartment.

Once again there was kissing—so much kissing—but Mateo pumped the brakes before it could go any farther. He was adamantly opposed to our doing anything more during my first two days in New York, and no matter how vociferously I argued, he refused to back down. The anticipation was the most beautiful kind of torture, whetting my appetite one brain-cell-liquefying kiss at a time. I was in awe of his level of control for two reasons.

First, I knew he'd had plenty of sex in his life. In addition to his one college girlfriend, I had a recollection of him being very social with the girls in high school. I'd even overheard my father counseling him on the importance of condom usage right around the time Mateo was a senior in high school. I remembered how embarrassed his voice had sounded when he promised he was using one every single time. I hadn't cared at the time, but in retrospect, I hated every single person he'd ever been intimate with because I was fun and rational like that.

The second reason I was amazed by his control was because I knew he wanted me as desperately as I wanted him. The way he held onto me was an education in desire. I could almost feel the desperation rolling off of him in waves. Somehow, he held himself in check, even as I did my best to topple his resistance.

We'd planned my visit strategically in order to use the least amount of Mateo's vacation days possible. In total, he would only be taking two long weekends and one "sick" day while I was there, which was ideal since the rest of his vacation days were allocated to coming to see me in Spain.

I hadn't been in town for a year, but having grown up there for most of my life, New York had become a second home to me. I spent the first two afternoons of my visit with two of my high school friends, Robin and Erica. The idea of me being with a man seemed to gross them out a little, which I thought was silly. After all, Mateo wasn't fifty. Robin thought it was crazy that we hadn't had sex yet—'how are you *still* a virgin' she'd asked, like I was a complete oddity. Even thought it was a bit uncomfortable at times it had still been nice to see them both and catch up—but I wasn't upset that they would both be busy for a lot of the time I was in town.

I'd thought about trying to extend an olive branch to my mother, only to decide against it. My whole life I'd had to take the high road with her. For once, I wanted her to make the effort to be the parent.

After a long day of shopping with Robin and Erica, I was happy to be home with Mateo. He and I were relaxing on the outdoor deck of the penthouse after an amazing dinner at a local Chinese restaurant. I was so obsessed with the food I quickly declared it to be our official go-to for future dinners.

Even though it was hot and muggy out, there was a certain beauty to Manhattan. I didn't love it as much as I loved Spain—I don't believe I loved any place that much—but I did thoroughly enjoy it. You couldn't replicate the thing that made New York what it was. The pulse of constant frenetic energy ran through the city at all times. The city never took a rest—there was always something going on, even in the dead of night.

"It's so gorgeous," I sighed happily as I leaned forward against the brick wall and stared down at the view from the outdoor patio area.

"That?" he laughed as wrapped his arms around me from behind. "No, mi bello amor. What is in front of you is not gorgeous. The only thing I see which fits that description is you."

I leaned back against his firm chest with a grin. Nothing made me happier than being with Mateo. As he shifted position behind me, I felt his arousal against my backside. I bit my lip to contain the choked sound of need that wanted to pass my lips. He hugged me tighter as he leaned in close, the stubble on his face sliding against my cheek.

"I am so happy to have you in my arms," he sighed.

"Knowing that you will be here when I get home from work each day is everything."

I wiggled against him as I turned around, smiling at his sharp inhale at the way I'd blatantly rubbed against his erection. Wrapping my arms around his torso, I looked up so we were eye to eye.

"I feel the same," I shared. "I want to be with you—"

"All of the time," we said in unison.

I threw my head back and laughed, the joy of the moment flooding my senses.

"We are on the same page," he said as his hands trailed from my waist back to my bottom.

I adored how possessive he was, loved the feral look in his eyes as he squeezed his hands and brought me in closer.

"Kiss me," I pleaded breathlessly.

His kisses were my entire world. There was no getting used to it so that it would become old hat to me, either. Every kiss felt just as monumental as it had the first time. I whimpered when he pulled back and rested his forehead against mine.

"I hate when you stop—"

My sentence was cut short when he lifted me up into his arms.

"Then tonight we will not stop," he murmured.

"Really?"

"No sex," he clarified, "but there are other things I can do to please you, mi tesoro."

I buried my face against the side of his neck, raining soft kisses from his earlobe to the top of his shirt. As much as I loved the kissing, I was desperate to touch and taste him everywhere. The strangled sound he made told me how much he liked what I was doing. Another clue was the haste with which he walked us to the bedroom. Setting me back on my feet next to the bed, he wrapped me up in his arms and kissed me again.

I yanked his button-down shirt up and out of his waistband and then slid one hand up under it so I could enjoy the warmth of his skin against my hand. His tongue lashed against mine as he kissed me desperately, moaning into my mouth as my hand slid up, up, up, only stopping when I reached his firm pectoral muscle. Putting my other hand beneath the shirt, I traced that hand up the other side before slowly gliding my hands back down.

His muscles rippled beneath my fingers as I made my way to the spot right below his bellybutton, where I felt the start of his happy trail. I traced it with my finger, sliding ever so slowly down until my journey was halted at the top of his pants. I gripped his belt in my hands, my thumbs fumbling as I blindly tried to undo it.

Mateo let out a tortured sound as he tore his mouth from mine, his breath coming in ragged bursts as he looked down into my eyes.

"If you go any further, I will come," he rasped. "I have been so desperate for you for so long that it will not take much to get me there."

I whimpered his name again as I rubbed against him. "I don't care. Touch me," I begged. "Just touch me."

He held me tighter as he plundered my mouth again, our tongues tangling frantically, the heat in the room seeming to rise exponentially. I was surprised when I felt the edge of his bed behind me since I hadn't realized we were moving. Mateo's fingers trailed along my midriff at the gap between my top and the waist of the skirt I had on, causing me to pull my mouth away as I arched further into his touch.

Both hands disappeared beneath the hem of my top, pulling it up inch by inch as he moved. He licked his lips and watched as more of my skin was exposed to his hungry gaze. "Eres tan hermosa."

I lifted my arms in the air, signaling that I wanted him to take my top off. "I think you're beautiful, too," I answered.

My world went dark for a second as the form-fitting olive colored top was pulled over my head. I laughed as he got it all the way off and tossed it aside without care. There was a built in bra sewn in, so once the shirt was gone, I was naked from the waist up. My nipples were peaked and my breasts felt heavy and needy for his touch.

His eyes traced over me like a caress. "My God, Avelina," he rasped.

My fingers went to the front of his shirt. "You too," I whispered.

He nodded but kept his eyes on me. I noticed his fingers weren't steady as he undid the buttons at lightning speed. When his perfectly bronzed skin was revealed, I bit my lip as I swayed toward him. Setting my hands against his bared stomach as he shrugged the shirt from his shoulders and let it drop to the floor. Unable to help myself I stepped in closer and set my nose down just above his belly button, inhaling softly as I traced his skin with it. I was so aroused by the blatant sensuality of his scent that I couldn't hold in the appreciative sigh I let out.

Mateo's hands threaded into my hair and tugged me back softly as I traced the spot over his heart with my tongue.

"Mi bello diablo," he said huskily.

Being called a beautiful devil wasn't an insult. I knew he'd said it because he was as affected as I was. He helped me up onto the bed before climbing on top of me, my legs spread around his thighs. He held my gaze, his emerald eyes a kaleidoscope of desire as he positioned his mouth above my left breast. His breath fanned out over me, the sensation causing my core to clench with need. My back arched off the bed when he flicked his tongue against my nipple several times in quick succession.

"Mat—"

My words gave way to a gasp as he sucked my nipple into his mouth. I felt and heard the rumble in his chest as he suckled and licked, the passion of his actions leaving me breathless. The way he worked my body and the certainty that he was as turned on as I was made it the headiest experience I'd ever had.

His attentions switched to my right breast, which was even more sensitive than my left. The feeling of his tongue on my skin made my heart beat faster than it ever had. As he worked his magic, I trailed my fingers over every inch of his exposed skin I could get to. I loved the raw strength I felt, loved the way he licked and nibbled harder when I traced certain areas. I filed each one away in a mental notebook, making sure to remember the spots that drove him wild.

I lost my breath as he began licking his way down my torso. "Your skin tastes like heaven," he groaned.

He trailed his tongue around my bellybutton before dipping it inside and wiggling, which made me gasp and giggle at the same time. When he tugged the elastic hem of my skirt down, his eyes caught mine as he touched the side of my bikini underwear at the same time. I nodded my consent to his unasked question and lifted my hips as he rolled the satin and my skirt down my legs.

It felt like the most natural thing in the world to be naked in front of him, which meant I wasn't feeling shy. When he let my skirt and underwear drop down to the floor and turned his attention to me, I didn't try to cover myself or look away because I knew what I needed—and what I wanted to share with him.

"Dios ayúdame."

The way he lapsed into Spanish when he was aroused enthralled me.

"God help you what?" I asked.

"Not come in the next minute like a teenager waking up from a wet dream," he answered. "You are a goddess, Ava. I want to touch, taste and lick every inch of your perfect silken skin."

"Then do it."

He needed no further invitation. He settled between my thighs, leaning in and rubbing his nose back and forth gently on my pubic bone as I trembled beneath him. I wasn't anxious about losing my virginity, but I couldn't say the same about oral sex. Those thoughts went right out the window when he began drawing a line with his tongue down my molten center.

For the briefest of moments his tongue fluttered against my clit, but in that time I lost every thought in my head. He trailed lower and swirled his tongue around as he put his hands behind my knees to press my legs out so I was totally open to him.

"Mateo!"

I felt his grumbled moan on my clit, the vibration making goose bumps break out all over my body. He was in total control as his tongue worked a wicked kind of magic I'd never suspected was possible. I went wild, my fingers threading through his thick locks as I held on and tried to remember to breathe. The feel of his stubble against my inner thighs was a surprising aphrodisiac.

I begged and pleaded for something I didn't understand. Yes, I'd touched myself before, but the way Mateo was making me feel was new. His hot tongue was everywhere, precisely where I needed it most at any given moment. When he sucked my clit into his mouth, I yelled out a broken string of nonsensical words and rocked my hips as I held his head right where I wanted it.

"That's it, that's it," I cried. "There!"

My legs locked and my back arched as an orgasm blasted through my body like a rocket ship. I stopped breathing for countless seconds as it went on and on, his tongue continuing to work magic on me. When it was finally over I was a sweaty trembling mess. Super-sensitive between my legs I yanked his head back and groaned.

"Please," I whimpered, "hold me."

Without hesitation he adjusted his position on the bed and rolled me over so I was on top of him, secure in his arms. I smiled when I heard his heart thundering beneath my ear. His scent was richer than ever before, and I realized it was because he was aroused.

His fingers caressed my scalp soothingly as he held me close. "Mi tesoro," he murmured, "nunca olvidaré esta noche.

I loved that he had called me his treasure.

"I'll never forget this night either," I murmured against his chest.

As I waited patiently for my breathing to return to normal, I began tracing broad circles across his stomach. With my cheek resting over his heart I was in prime position to view his erection, and I kept biting my lip as I tried to decide what to do. Tilting my head back I looked up to Mateo.

"Kiss me."

He shifted position so that we were face-to-face on our sides. Cupping the left side of my cheek with his palm, he leaned in and did as I asked. I tasted myself in his kiss, but it didn't bother me at all. His tongue and my own immediately started the dance that only the two of us knew the steps to, working in perfect rhythm as we explored each other.

I had to force myself not to get lost in it, which was hard. Only my desire to touch him made it possible. I worked my right hand between us and cupped his erection through his slacks, smiling when he ripped his mouth from mine and let out a tortured sounding groan. I exhaled a sound of annoyance as fingers fumbled with his belt, unable to get it undone. His breath came out in ragged gusts as he helped me, pulling the belt off and throwing it over his shoulder. He helped me with the button of his pants, but I smacked his hand away when he went for the zipper.

"Let me open my own present," I teased.

His smile made my core clench with need. Even though I'd just come, I wanted more. Pulling down the zipper, I reached in and touched the elastic waistband of his boxer briefs. He made a choked sound but didn't stop me as I worked his erection out. My eyes widened as I took in the long and thick perfection before me, my mouth watering with the desire to taste him like he'd tasted me. I let out a little sound of my own when I saw the head was wet with pre-cum. I ran my fingers through it, gathering it so I could spread it up and down his shaft.

"Ava, please," he begged huskily. "Fuck!"

My confidence grew in leaps and bounds. Mateo didn't curse much around me. That he had dropped the F word let me know he was losing control. I gripped him firmly and began shuttling my fist up and down his length. He rolled onto this back as he moaned something in Spanish I didn't quite catch. As I pumped, he thrust his hips up over and over again.

"Ava, Ava, Ava," he rasped my name like a prayer on his lips.

With his eyes closed and his head arched back I took the opportunity to surprise him. Sitting up, I slid down the bed until I was in the right position. Bringing my face down over him, I traced my tongue across the fat head of his erection.

"Carajo, Ava, por favor!"

Again with the use of the F word only this time it was in Spanish. Emboldened by his plea, I fisted the bottom of his shaft and opened my mouth to draw the head in. Inch by inch I worked my way down as Mateo alternately praised and begged me in a mixture of Spanish and English.

In Spanish, he asked me to take him deep—*Más profundo*—as he put my head in his hands and helped guide my motions.

My mouth was split wide with him as I worked my way as far down as I could before he hit the back of my throat, which was just shy of half way. His obvious pleasure urged me on, and I lost any inhibition as I bobbed my head up and down on his shaft. The room was full of the sound of my mouth on him and it was XXX rated. Never had I realized that giving a blowjob would be so wild and loud. Instead of finding it offensive, I loved it. Even better, I could tell he did, too.

"Me voy a venir," he rasped as his back arched and he tried to guide my mouth off of him.

Instead of allowing him to do so, I sucked harder.

"Me voy a venir en tu boca si no te detienes," he choked, telling me again that he was going to come—and if I didn't stop, it would be in my mouth.

Since I wanted him to finish that way, I did not heed his warnings. He let out a broken groan as he stiffened beneath me and came, his hot seed pouring into my mouth. There was so much that some dripped out of the side of my mouth when I couldn't swallow fast enough. When he was finished, I pulled my mouth off slowly, swallowing the rest before wiping the side of my lips and licking my fingers.

Mateo's eyes blazed into mine as he pulled me down on top of him.

"You will be the death of me," he rasped as he held me close.

"What a way to go," I joked.

He chuckled, the sound rumbling beneath the ear I had to his chest. "The best way, I would think," he murmured.

We fell asleep just like that. Some time later he woke me up and got us into bed properly. I went back to sleep with a smile on my face.

# Ten

*Ava—3 years ago*

THE WEEK THAT FOLLOWED AFTER THE FIRST night we'd gotten truly intimate had been one of discovery. Mateo was still adamant about not having sex, but everything else was on the table. I spent my days anxiously anticipating the hours between when he came home from work and when we would fall asleep in each other's arms, sated and exhausted.

One of Mateo's college friends was allowing us to use his beachfront vacation home in the Hamptons while he and his family were in Greece and I was crazy excited about it. I knew four uninterrupted days with Mateo was going to be phenomenal. We'd packed together on Wednesday night so we'd be ready to go when he came home from work at lunch on Thursday.

We'd fully intended to go the instant he came home but then we saw each other and one thing led to another. Needless to say, it was another hour before we got out of the apartment but that was okay since both of us were completely blissed out.

Mateo drove us out to the Hamptons in his dark blue convertible Mercedes E550. The one thing I didn't miss about Spain was the security. It was nice to be able to be totally alone with no one following along after us. I knew that once Mateo started working at Cruz Saez that would change, but until then I planned to thoroughly enjoy the freedom.

When we got into town, we stopped at the supermarket and did some quick shopping. After we had finished up there, we drove through town with the top down on our way to his friend's home. The sky was a perfect sunshine soaked blue with a few fluffy clouds spread out as far as the eye could see. I found myself relaxing easily into the beach atmosphere, thoroughly embracing the salty scent of sea and sand that hung in the air. The most recent Bruno Mars album played on the radio as I took photos of dunes, sea grass and Mateo at the wheel. The way the wind whipped his hair around was just about the sexiest thing ever and seeing him so relaxed and happy made everything perfect. He steered the car with his left hand while his right rested on my thigh, just another reminder of the connection we shared. I took several photos to document it all, knowing I'd want to remember it forever.

We pulled up to the house just after four. It was a large house on one of the quiet beach roads that didn't allow parking along the side of the road. That meant it was a nice and quiet area with no crowds. The interior of the house was lovely and the view of the ocean was gorgeous. One of the decks had an inviting looking blue pool while the level below led out to a long walkway straight to the beach. We made quick work of unpacking the car and putting the groceries away and then separated so Mateo could take the top off the hot tub for us. I used the time to explore the house, going from room to room to see the view from different spots.

My favorite part of the house bar none was the master bedroom. The bed faced a wall of glass that led out to the deck overlooking the sea. I flung the French doors open and inhaled the ocean air, smiling as the sound of waves crashing filled the air. I had always loved the beach but being there with Mateo was even more special. I knew the memories we made would last a lifetime.

"I like seeing this smile on your face," he said from beside me. "You love this view, do you not?"

I grinned bigger as I turned to face him. "The view is wonderful, but that's not what's got me so happy. I'm excited it's just the two of us with no work and no computer for four whole days. It's a lot to smile about."

Mateo chuckled as he slid his arms around my waist. "We could buy a house of our own here on the beach so we can do more getaways like this in the future."

I tilted my head back so we were looking right at each other. "Really?"

"What my treasure wants, she gets."

"I just want you," I said softly. "You're absolutely necessary. Everything else is just a perk."

He groaned as he buried his face in my hair. "So much beauty, inside and out."

Before I could respond he'd lifted his head and was using his two fingers at my chin to tilt mine back. His mouth covered mine softly, his tongue teasing along the seam of my lips until I opened and flicked my tongue against his. Just like that, things went from sweet to sensual. Reaching up I linked my fingers behind his neck, moaning when he slanted his head to the other side and kissed me even more passionately. I moaned and wrapped my legs around him when he put his hands beneath my buttocks and hoisted me up against him.

The feeling of his thick erection pressed up against my panty-covered sex was to die for. I rocked against him shamelessly; loving the tension I could feel in his body, as he held on tight and kissed me like he'd never, ever get enough. Our kiss grew hotter and deeper, the sound of our rapid breathing mixing with the crashing of the waves on the beach in the background.

I tore my mouth away and buried my face in his neck as he guided me back and forth against him. He rubbed against the perfect spot each time he brought me forward and I could feel myself unraveling fast. I nibbled along his neck then soothed each spot with a tender lick as I ground against him. When I gently bit down on his earlobe and flicked my tongue against it, he let out a string of rapid-fire Spanish pleas. Keeping my arms around his neck, I arched my back and leaned out, watching his face as he moved my hips.

"You make me feel so good," I whimpered.

"Tu cuerpo sabe lo que quiere," he answered huskily.

He was right—my body knew exactly what it wanted—ed. Namely a six-foot-plus Spanish man who kissed like a god and made me happier than I'd ever known I could be. He kept me against him as he shut the French doors and pulled the curtains closed before setting me down on the bed and rocking my world. It was the best start to a vacation I'd ever had.

We grilled steak, corn, and baked potatoes for dinner and ate out on the patio, the ocean the perfect soundtrack for the meal. As was our way, we sat right next to one another. Mateo liked to share his food with me, holding out his fork to me with cuts of steak he deemed to be the best.

After dinner and clean up we went down to the ocean and walked along the surf. I laughed as the tide lapped against my ankles. The water was just a bit warmer than it was in Barcelona, which I found enjoyable. From time to time I would ask Mateo to hand me the camera I'd asked him to hold onto for me so I wouldn't drop it in the water. We took a slew of selfies of us together, all of which he had to take since his arms were longer. I joked we needed a photographer to do it for us and he declared he would find someone to take photos of us together before we left.

As the sun was setting, I walked backward to capture him in the fading light. I knew the pictures would be keepers because he looked delicious—his white tee shirt accented his perfect chest and his hair blew across his forehead highlighting those gorgeous green eyes.

"I think you have got enough of me. Now it is my turn, mi bello amor. Give me the camera," he laughed.

I handed it over with one of my own, running ahead of him again as I kicked at the surf. Turning back I looked over my shoulder at him with a saucy look. His steps picked up speed as he made a low growly sound. I danced in and out of the surf, letting it lap against my shins as

I smiled and posed for every photo he wanted to take. When he'd taken no fewer than two-dozen, he caught up to me and hauled me into his arms.

"We buy a house here immediately," he announced. "I love seeing you happy and free like this."

I stood on my tiptoes and kissed him softly. "All you need to do is stay by my side. I'm this way whenever I'm with you—it doesn't matter where we are."

He grinned as he stepped back and slung the camera around his neck before turning around. "Hop up so we can make our way back to the house."

He didn't need to ask me twice. When he bent his knees so I'd have an easier time of it I braced my hands on his shoulders and hopped on. Wrapping my legs around his waist and my arms around his shoulders, I rubbed my face against the side of his as he began walking.

"All this *and* a personal carrier to transport me from place to place?" I teased. "This really is the best vacation ever."

He laughed as he rubbed his warm hands along the bottom of my legs. "If you wish, I will gladly carry you wherever you wish to go."

"I just want to be wherever you are," I answered honestly.

He squeezed my legs softly and sighed. "I have dreamt of being with you like this hundreds of times, but none of them ever matched up to this reality. Everything is better, brighter, bigger... I could not ask for more. You are everything, Avelina. My entire world revolves around you."

I was glad he couldn't see my over-the-top dorky grin because I had a feeling I looked like a complete loon.

When we got back to the house I stayed on his back as he turned out the lights before walking us into the bedroom. Once we got there, he turned around and backed up to the bed so I could get down. I wasn't graceful about it at all, instead plopping back onto the bed with a chuckle as I let go of my lock around his shoulders and waist. Mateo turned around with a grin that quickly turned into a look of desire as his eyes trailed over my body. The skirt of my white halter style dress lay across my upper thighs, dangerously close to exposing my underwear to him. Propping myself up on my elbows, I fluttered my eyelashes at him dramatically.

"Hi there, handsome."

"Mira lo hermosa que eres," he murmured, lifting the camera from around his neck and turning it on.

"What're you doing?" I laughed.

"Before and after," he answered huskily, the sound of the SDR camera shutter whirring as he took several photos of my face.

"Before and after what?" I asked.

He set the camera aside and traced his fingers up the inside of my legs from my knees up to my thighs.

"Before I make love to you, and after."

My breath caught in my throat as my heartbeat began racing at triple speed.

"Really?"

He crawled up on the bed and positioned himself over me so we were face to face.

"Sí," he nodded, his nose rubbing softly against mine as he did.

I had two seconds to beam up at him like a demented

137

prom queen before he kissed me with such passion I lost my breath. I wanted to be with him so badly I ached with it. The very idea of having Mateo inside of me made me emotional in the best way.

I lifted my legs and wrapped them around his hips, pulling him in closer as my hands threaded into his hair. He groaned and used his free hand to pull my skirt up to my waist while he rubbed against me just so. Tearing his mouth away from mine, he looked down at me with passion filled eyes.

"I want this dress off," he said thickly.

I nodded, unwrapping myself from him before taking the hand he held out to help me sit up. Gripping the hem of my dress, he raised it up and over my head. I favored clothing with bras built in which meant there was nothing else to remove but my underwear once the dress was off. I stood from the bed so that I was right in front of him. I smiled at him as I unbuttoned and unzipped his cargo shorts and let them fall to the floor before he pulled his tee shirt up and over his head.

Over the course of the previous days, we'd quickly found that we both very much enjoyed being naked together. I didn't have any shame in my body around Mateo—how could I when he looked at me as if I'd been created just for him? He had no qualms about being undressed in front of me, either. That worked for me since I wanted to see him that way all of the time. I tugged at the waistband of his boxer briefs before pulling them down, licking my lips when his erection sprang free.

Anxious to touch him, I dropped to my knees and helped him take his briefs off all the way. He kicked them impatiently to the side when I leaned forward and licked the underside of his throbbing head. He groaned low in his throat as his right hand slid into my hair.

"I love watching you do this," he murmured.

I fisted the lower portion of him in my right hand as I trailed my tongue over the head before opening my mouth and pulling him in. Applying suction, I worked myself back and forth on him.

"Your perfect little mouth looks so good wrapped around my dick," he said huskily.

My thighs clenched as I watched him watching me suck him. The hand in my hair gripped tighter as I picked up the pace. When I pulled him out and tapped the head against my tongue, he let out a harsh sound as a shot of pre-cum splattered against my tongue.

I took him back into my mouth and laved the head with my tongue as his eyes blazed down into mine.

"Tan bueno, Ava."

I nodded my head and moaned around his thick shaft, then let out a squeak of surprise when he pulled away. With no fanfare, he lifted me up and tossed me on the bed, yanking my white lace underwear off with lightning speed.

"I have to taste you," he said.

That was all the warning I got before my legs were spread around his shoulders and his tongue was all over me, not that I was complaining. The hot slide of his velvety tongue against me was a delicious agony I never wanted to end but also wanted it to take me over the edge. He slid one finger inside and I cried out as I fisted the comforter beneath me.

I whimpered when he lifted his head and stopped moving his tongue.

"You are so tight against just the one finger," he said as he pulled it out slowly. "How will you do with two?"

His question didn't require an answer since he immediately covered me with his mouth again and began rolling his tongue against my clit in a circular motion. I called out his name as he slid his fingers in and out, in and out, all while continuing the motions with his tongue. My heels dug into his back as I came with a series of breathless cries.

He kept his fingers inside as he propped himself up over me and leaned in for a kiss. We went at each other savagely, the kiss wild and uninhibited as he continued moving his fingers in and out. He built me back up one moment at a time only to pull his fingers out right as I was building up to another orgasm.

"Please," I begged as he broke the kiss and sat back on his haunches.

"What do you want, mi tesoro?"

"I want you inside of me," I whimpered as I put my hands on his back and ran my nails down to his backside.

He fisted himself tight and positioned himself against me, rubbing the head against me teasingly.

"So wet," he murmured. "Your body is ready, Ava, but this will hurt. If there was another way..."

I dug my nails into his ass as I pulled him closer. "Do it," I whispered. "I want all of me to be yours. The pain will pass."

He nodded and then kissed me as he ever so slowly began working his way inside. Once he'd fed an inch inside, he no longer needed to hold the base of his shaft, which left that hand free for something else. I moaned into his mouth as he began rubbing my clit. My body seemed to know what to do, my hips naturally tilting to take him in deeper.

We tore our mouths apart when he hit the barrier. He was breathing like he was mid-marathon, which was crazy hot. I clenched around him and moaned his name as he stayed exactly where he was, not moving an inch as he stared into my eyes.

"Why aren't you moving?" I asked breathlessly.

"There is one more part of the before," he answered.

I shook my head and wiggled myself on him.

"Wha—what?"

His fingers stopped moving just before he set his hand on my waist to hold me still.

"I want to tell you something important before we take this step. Decades from now when we are married with a house full of children, we will remember this moment."

When he said we would be married, my heart almost exploded with pure joy.

"Tell me," I whispered.

His emerald eyes held mine as he spoke. "Te amo mas de lo que nunca sabras."

He'd told me he loved me more than I would ever know.

I sniffled and blinked back tears. I'd known he loved me because I could feel it and see it in all of his actions, but it was the first time he was saying it out loud.

"I love you just as much," I answered.

"Por siempre," he said as he set his forehead against mine.

I nodded. "Forever," I agreed.

Anything else I might have said was lost when he surged into me with one hard thrust.

I yelped at the pain and dug my nails into his backside, the stinging sensation uncomfortable. Mateo seemed to know exactly what I needed, staying stock still over me as I adjusted to him.

He smiled down at me softly, his eyes full of so much love I couldn't help but see it.

"Mi amante," I whispered, calling him my lover in Spanish.

His smile was huge as he nodded. "Mi bello amor."

Ever so slowly he began to retreat, only to slide forward when he was almost all the way out. At first I struggled to relax because I felt so overly full. When he started rubbing circles against my clit again it didn't take me long to get into it. He stayed low on top of me as he thrust in and out, our mouths fusing in a passionate kiss as he made love to me. I broke the kiss when it got to be too much. I started whimpering and pleading for him to make me come and he nodded his understanding. The pads of his fingers pressed down on my clit more firmly as he pushed deep, hitting something inside of me that made me light up.

I threw my head back and cried out his name as I clenched around his shaft and came. His rough cry came as I was riding my own release out and the hot feeling of his come inside of me made me clench around him harder. I hadn't known that would feel as good as it did and I was glad I'd gotten on birth control so we could be together without condoms.

"Avelina," he roared as he thrust inside one last time and locked up, his entire body trembling as his shaft jerked inside of me.

After he finished he relaxed on top of me for almost a minute, breathing too hard to say anything. I held him tight, enjoying the feeling of him being over me while also being deep inside. When he was able to take a deep breath he rolled onto his back, taking me with him.

I laid on his chest drowsily as he pushed sweat-dampened hair off my forehead before tracing a finger down my cheek.

"That was everything," he said.

"Everything and more," I agreed.

We stayed like that for a few minutes before he lifted me off and laid me on my back. Lifting up the camera again, he stood over me.

"Just your face," he assured me.

I nodded, never having thought for even a second he would start snapping nudes. He took several shots before declaring that he'd gotten it perfect. Setting the camera down, he lifted me up and carried me into the bathroom so we could wash up.

I went to bed that night sore but over-the-moon happy and so in love I knew nothing would ever come between us.

# Eleven

*Mateo—present*

After retreating from the apartment, I went to work for a few hours and tried to be productive. It should have been easy since the only staff there was the nighttime cleaning crew, but I could not get my head in the game. This was not a surprise since I had been a mess in my head for months.

I was hanging by a thread and I knew it. It was part of the reason I had brought Ava home the way I did. Of course I knew she had not been on a date—I had had every person she interacted with vetted to make certain they were not a threat. The truth was that I had needed her back so badly that when she went to dinner and I realized the opportunity before me, I jumped without another thought. I could barely breathe without her by my side. Where she was concerned I could never turn my emotions off. I would not want to, either.

Once I gave up on trying to work, my next stop was my brother's. My anxiety was at an all-time high and I was not focused, which was why weeks prior, Alejandro had come to New York to help me out at work. What that really meant was he had come to monitor me, and not just at work. My entire family was beside themselves about what was going on with Avelina and things were harder for them because they were also justifiably worried about how I was doing physically and emotionally.

I had to admit it was smart of them to have sent him. I had been a wreck when he arrived- not eating, barely sleeping and unable to focus on anything other than how wrecked my life was. Jandro had stepped up and kicked my ass into shape, reminding me that I had to stay strong for Ava, if for no other reason.

"You have to believe she will find her way back," he said. "I sure as hell do. You two love each other more than any other couple I've ever seen."

I half-smiled at Alejandro but could not put all that much into it. I did not currently see much to be happy about.

"It is hard when she is so angry with me for things she knows I did not do. Tonight for the first time I feared that the wall she has erected is insurmountable. It kills me to watch her doubt me."

"Things are twisted in her head, but it will resolve itself. Her therapist has said things are a little better."

I blew out a frustrated breath and shook my head as I gripped the mug of coffee in my hand. "She has, but that is all she is able to tell me without violating Ava's rights."

"The doctor would not have given you hope if there weren't any," Alejandro asserted. "Things are better than they were, Mateo. You said yourself she has put on four pounds and she no longer looks like she's about to drop at any moment."

He was right. I was proud of her small weight gain and relieved that the dark circles beneath her eyes were no longer purplish black. Still, it twisted me up inside that she had only made progress after I let her think I was letting her go. The woman I fell in love with would never have believed any lies about me for a moment—nor would she have considered a separation for any length of time. Before the accident, being apart for ten hours a day to work had been inconvenient. Days would have been painful; weeks would have been out of the question.

I swallowed thickly and looked away from my brother's assessing eyes. "Having her look at me with anger instead of love is ripping me apart inside, Jandro. I can not help fear it will never change."

I felt him behind me right before he set his hand down on my shoulder. "This will pass, brother. The trauma she has been through messed with her mind, but it cannot permanently change who she is. Underneath it all, she is still a fighter. She just needs to remember it."

"How do I get her to do that? You should have seen her face when I asked her if she remembered. She looked at me as though I had plunged a knife into her chest."

He sighed and leaned across the counter. "The stress of the last year would be enough to bring anyone down to the mat for a while. The accident happening after all of that was more than she could take. I know you understand why she doesn't want to remember that day in particular."

My stomach cramped painfully as a highlight reel of

that day rolled through my mind. The moment the police called to tell me there had been an accident was embedded in my brain for eternity.

"If I could forget that day and what came after, I would do it in an instant—but not if it meant losing her. It tears at my soul that she is purposely forgetting things in order to push me away."

"She isn't doing it to push *you* away," he reminded me. "The doctors have told you it is a psychological defense mechanism to protect herself from what she doesn't want to recall. Once she remembers the whole day, that will change."

"That is what they tell me," I agreed.

"Don't you dare give up," Alejandro said firmly. "She is going to come back to herself."

That thought was the only thing that kept me going on any given day but after how badly things had gone in the kitchen earlier, I had to wonder if I was fooling myself.

"I will never give up, but I can not help fear that it will not matter in the end. Even showing her the evidence is a risk because she could hate me for forcing the reality on her. For right now I just need to get over today and get back home."

"Be patient. It will happen."

I sighed and nodded my head. "I will endeavor to be even more patient," I sighed. A quick look at my watch showed I had been out of the apartment for almost five hours. Pushing my coffee mug away, I stood from the stool at his counter.

"I need to get back."

When we got to the front door Jandro stopped me.

"I know this is going to sound crazy, but you need to give her some space, brother."

My head reared back in surprise. "I just gave her nine weeks of space," I snapped.

"Yes, and now you've brought her back. Give her a little room to adjust to that. She is still not herself, Mateo."

My brother's words humbled me because he had a point. After steering clear of her for nine weeks I had burst onto the scene like a bat out of hell. No wonder she was so angry and overwhelmed. More than ever, she needed me to be strong for her.

I nodded as I exhaled slowly. "I will be patient and give her space to adjust to being back."

"It'll all work out," he said as he clapped me on the shoulder and sent me on my way.

After I left my brother's, I had my driver take me to a small market not far from the house. Grabbing a cart, I made my way up and down the aisles picking up groceries. I might not be able to get her to remember, but I could damn well make sure there was food in the house for her. I had wanted to kick myself when I found her in the kitchen looking at the empty refrigerator.

I got back home after midnight, entering quietly with a ton of reusable shopping bags slung over each arm. I was almost into the kitchen when I heard a sound behind me. Turning, I saw Avelina had fallen asleep on one of the sofas. Needing to get the bags off my arms, I left her there and set about putting the groceries away. I thought for sure she would wake up as I moved around, but that did not happen.

When I was finished putting everything away, I went

to the couch she was asleep on and crouched down in front of her. Up close I saw tear tracks and realized she had cried herself to sleep. The only light in the room was coming from the television, which was muted and tuned to a home shopping channel. Picturing her crying while staring at someone selling kitchen gadgets was like a punch to the stomach.

I said her name, twice, but got no response, so I decided to let her sleep. Standing, I bent over and lifted her up into my arms. The weight of her in my arms was too damn light, which bothered me. As I walked toward the master bedroom, the scent of her mango bath products made me hard. I had missed the scent and taste of her so much it nearly drove me insane. She would never know how much it cost me to let her leave and try to start a life in Jersey. Even though I had known it would not be permanent, it had not mattered. Being without her was hell.

With her clutched close, I opened the door to the bedroom and walked toward the bed. A lamp on the dresser across the room was the only sign anyone had been in the room recently. Other than the cleaners and the team who had unpacked her things in the closet earlier, no one had been in the room since the furniture and décor had been put in. Grabbing the top of the comforter, I pulled it down so I could put her on the bed.

The idea was to do it fast, like ripping a Band-Aid off, but I had been deprived of her in my arms for so long that I could not. Instead, I sat down on the bed and carefully maneuvered myself until my back was against the propped up pillows in front of the headboard. It was awkward positioning myself with only one arm since she was lying across the other, but I did it.

I promised myself I would hold her for a few minutes and then I would leave. My heart stopped when she sighed as she leaned into me and set her head down on my shoulder. Lifting her free arm, she draped it around my torso before going lax against me. It hit me that in her sleep she instinctively turned to and trusted me. I hoped that was a good sign of things to come.

I held tight and savored having her in my arms where she belonged. Unable to keep my eyes open, I fell into a deep and uninterrupted sleep that did not include nightmares for the first time in months. By the grace of God, I woke up around five in the morning. We had naturally assumed our customary position—legs tangled together, and her face against my chest. I knew if she had awakened to find me in bed with her, she would have been furious. It was like Mission Impossible getting out of the bed without disturbing her. Once I was out, I practically moonwalked from the room so she wouldn't wake up and realize I had been there most of the night.

I could not find it in me to regret holding her for those hours.

# Twelve

*Ava-Present*

My nerves were stretched pretty thin from being under the same roof with Mateo for two days especially since we hadn't spoken much at all on day two. I'd been certain he would be right on top of me, but just the opposite was true. The whole thing had me on tenterhooks. On day one he'd been like a bull in an antique store. After our fight in the kitchen, he'd done a complete three-sixty and I wasn't happy about it. The only words we exchanged on my first full morning in the apartment happened when he came to tell me when my dress fitting was. I started to argue with him about it, but he wasn't having it. Rather than argue, he turned and went back to his home office, shutting the door after him as he did.

I spent the majority of my day out by the pool reading. It was strange not to go to work, although I couldn't say that was a bad thing. The job hadn't been my ideal, so I never got attached. It was a safe place to land, nothing more and nothing less than that. Still, it had given me something to focus on aside from the mess of my life. Now that I was once occupying the same space as Mateo, the treasure trove of things I was avoiding felt like it was bursting at the seams.

Earlier that morning I'd noticed he'd filled up the refrigerator with fruits, vegetables, milk and eggs. Not long after breakfast, one of his assistants arrived with meat, fish and chicken and a selection of cheeses. As the afternoon sun moved across the patio, I decided I'd hid behind my Kindle long enough and decided to make dinner. I admit I did this knowing it would lure Mateo out of his cave, and I further admit this was because his silence had me on edge. He did not, as a general rule, do the silent treatment. Mateo was a talker, not one to hold things in or bury emotions. That he'd stayed in the apartment instead of going to the office should've meant I saw plenty of him—but just the opposite was true. In the past when he worked from home, he left the door open at all times. Throughout the day I'd go in or he'd come out, both of us always happy to accrue all the time together we possibly could. It wasn't so much that I wanted to talk to or see him, I assured myself. It was the damn closed door that was throwing me off. That had to be it. If he'd just left it open as usual, I was certain I would've been able to ignore him without issue.

With my mind made up about cooking, I carried my stuff in from the pool and then took a quick shower to wash the mix of chlorine and sunscreen from my skin. Knowing I'd be making a mess in the kitchen, I didn't bother with my appearance. After quickly braiding my damp hair, I dressed in black yoga pants, a matching tank top and a pair of aqua-colored flip-flops. Once in the kitchen I grabbed my cheery red apron and set to pulling ingredients for chicken parmigiana.

I wasn't quiet as I cooked—it would have been impossible to be when I was pounding out chicken cutlets. Normally Mateo would have come out of his office to visit, but that wasn't happening. The damn door stayed closed like it was cemented shut, which only served to rattle me more. What was the point of forcing me to move in if he was going to ignore me?

After I got the fried cutlets onto a tray with sauce and cheese, I slid it and a loaf of garlic bread into the oven and then tossed some fresh pasta into boiling water. With everything pretty well set, I started making a salad. My frustration grew as I cleaned and chopped the lettuce, cucumbers and tomatoes because vegetable chopping was *his* job. Asshole.

Dinner was plated and on the table and still there wasn't a peep from him. With my annoyance firing me up, I stomped down the hall to his office and banged on the door.

"Come in."

I turned the knob and shoved the door open, gritting my teeth when I saw he was sitting behind the desk staring at me expectantly. He looked a little rough and his hair was a mess, which meant he'd been running his hands through it all day. Not that it mattered—even when he looked tired, he was still gorgeous. It really wasn't fair.

"I made dinner."

"Okay."

My eyes widened when he turned to face his computer screen and began typing.

"Are you not going to eat it?" I snapped.

He sighed, rolling his neck on his shoulders as he pushed back from the desk.

"It is best for us both to do our own thing for a while," he answered. "You are angry and my presence only seems to make it worse. I will steer clear while you adjust to being home."

My jaw dropped in shock. "If you wanted to avoid me, you should have left me in Jersey City!"

His eyes closed as he took and then released a big breath. When he opened them again, his expression was blank.

"You belong home," he ground out. "I am staying away not because I want to, but because I do not want to upset you or argue. I thought you would be thrilled."

It felt like pure ice was flowing through my veins. "Right. Well. I'm *thrilled* with your concern for my feelings. The leftovers will be in the fridge," I snapped before stepping out and closing the door behind me.

The food I had spent hours making tasted like ash, and I had to force myself to eat a quarter of it. Giving up, I scraped the remainder of my plate into the trash and set about cleaning up the kitchen. With nothing to do but sit in the apartment in silence, I went to the bedroom, changed my flip-flops out for a pair of Chucks and then pulled on a tee shirt over my tank top. Mateo's security team had an office on the ground floor of the building so I called down and asked for a car, then grabbed my purse and left the apartment.

When I settled into the car, I stopped dead when I saw the driver.

"You!" I gasped.

He had been my morning Uber driver to work the entire time I lived in Jersey City.

"You never worked for Uber at all, did you?"

He had the good grace to look away as he shook his head. "No ma'am."

My mind was reeling as the implications of his words hit me. "So the other drivers I saw weren't Uber either?"

"No."

I wondered who else I'd thought was just an average person had actually been on Mateo's payroll. I had a half a mind to stomp back upstairs and call him out for it, but I knew it would be pointless. He'd told me the day before that I'd had a security detail and he'd had no shame about it at all. When it came to safety, Mateo was unbendable, especially after my accident. He was correct when he'd noted that if I'd been thinking straight, I would have known he never would have sat back and let me live without security.

I let out a breath and forced myself to let it go. Leaning back in my seat, I told the driver to take me to the movies. I couldn't tell you what I saw since I bought a ticket for the next movie that was starting. It was a thriller, which meant a ton of crap blew up and twenty million rounds were fired. When it was over I went back to the lobby and bought a ticket for the next show. I retained nothing from that one, either.

The apartment was silent when I got back home. A quick perusal of the refrigerator told me Mateo had eaten at some point. Walking down the hall to the bedroom, I noticed the light under his office door was still on. By then it was well after ten at night, so I was surprised he was still in there.

As I prepared for bed the anxiety of having to try my gown on the next morning hit me hard. I tried reading, but couldn't get into anything. Next, I tried to watch television, but nothing caught my attention. I finally fell into a fitful sleep around midnight.

Just after three thirty in the morning, I woke up and couldn't get back to sleep. After half an hour of trying, I let out an aggrieved sigh and gave in. Pulling on my robe, I quietly made my way out of the bedroom with the intention of going to the kitchen to make a cup of warm milk. That all went out the window when I saw the light coming out from under the door of Mateo's office. I couldn't recall a time when he'd worked so much and as much as I didn't want to admit it to myself, I was worried.

Unable to ignore it, I went to the door and knocked softly.

"Come in."

When I opened the door, I realized he wasn't at the desk. I turned to the right and found him in the small sitting area he had for visitors at the back of the room. He was still dressed as he had been when I'd seen him hours earlier. His black tee shirt stretched across his broad shoulders, accenting his body as opposed to merely covering it. His lower half was covered in well-worn jeans fit him perfectly. Leaning back in the chair with his legs kicked out and crossed at the ankle, he looked like a mountain my traitorous body wanted to climb. He also looked exhausted.

"Why are you up?" he asked, not unkindly.

"I, uh, milk," I stammered. Taking a deep breath, I tried again. "I woke up and couldn't get back to sleep. I was on my way to the kitchen to make some warm milk and I saw your light on. What's your excuse?"

He cocked his head and stared at me silently for countless seconds.

His lack of response stung. "Never mind," I huffed.

"I do not sleep much anymore," he said.

My heart felt as though it were being squeezed by iron fists.

"Why?"

"Ava," he sighed tiredly, "why do you ask when you already know the answer?"

"How could I possibly know the reason?"

His jaw clenched as he stared at me with a look of exasperation. Setting his hands on the arms of the leather chair he was in, he pushed himself up and then walked to me.

"How have you been sleeping since the accident?" he asked.

A frisson of alarm skittered up my spine. We couldn't talk about that. If he tried to, I was prepared to run.

"I don't want to talk about—"

"I will take that as an acknowledgment that the answer is not well. Do you really imagine I sleep like a baby without you? I am tired all of the time, so tired I feel I am watching things around me from afar. That is what this life is now, no? I am never really awake anymore. Since that day, I have been stuck in this nightmare like a hamster on a goddamn wheel."

My hand went to my throat as I stared up at him. It was like having blinders removed. I'd thought he looked tired when he walked into my office the day before, but up close I could see it was much more than that. He was so exhausted there were dark circles beneath his eyes. I knew it was my fault.

I was hit with a memory of the antiseptic smell of the hospital and the sound of medical equipment. *"Wake up, mi tesoro. Please. Come back to me."*

I shook my head frantically and stepped back from him so fast I almost tripped over my feet.

"I have to go," I squeaked before turning on my heel and sprinting from the room.

When I got back to the bedroom, I closed and locked the door behind me like it could keep my memories shut out. I didn't fall back to sleep until the sun was coming up.

Just before nine the following morning he appeared as I was sitting down to breakfast. Once again he did not speak, instead choosing to sit at the counter where he pretended to be reading the newspaper. Really, he was watching me out of the corner of his eye. When I finished the bowl of oatmeal I'd made, he got up and left the room without a word.

I was relieved he didn't try to go with me to the dress fitting. I probably would have melted down if he had since I was more shaken than ever after our middle of the night exchange. I went by myself, taken by a driver and a member of the security team, both who sat in the front while I was taken back to the dressing area.

My eyes watered when I stepped into the dressing room and saw my gown hanging against the wall. My anxiety kicked up several notches but I managed to breathe through it as I undressed and allowed the seamstress to get me into it.

Of course, it was much looser than it was meant to be. The seamstress informed me that my fiancé had assured her I would be gaining weight over the course of the coming weeks. Therefore, she said she was going to fit it a little big. She assured me that ten days before the wedding it would be fitted again and at that time it would be tailored to fit perfectly.

Somehow I stayed calm during the process of measuring and pinning the dress. I did my best not to look at myself in the mirror because it made things too real for me. Not that it mattered much, I mean I was standing there in my wedding gown. It was a dress I'd bought specifically for him, at a time when I was beyond excited to become Mateo's wife. Putting it back on for a fitting was a reminder of how far off the rails my life had gone in such a short amount of time.

The seamstress went about her business quietly—annoyingly so, in my opinion. The silence allowed me to reflect the day that I bought the dress.

My father and Camila had gone with me to the dress shop in Barcelona and I'd tried on six dresses before I found the one. Each of the previous dresses had been too poufy, too tight, too shimmery or too plain. Dress seven was just right. I knew I was being difficult, but it was about so much more than the dress to me. I so badly wanted everything to be perfect for my father.

*Papá and Camila both gasped when I walked out from the dressing area.*

*"That is the one, mi ángel. You are all lit up inside and the smile on your face is exactly what I wanted to see," Papá said proudly.*

*Camila wiped tears away as she nodded. "Your father is right, sweetheart. This dress is perfection. You look like a princess."*

*I slowly turned around on the riser I was on, watching myself in the mirrors as I did.*

*"Yes," I agreed with a smile. "This is it. I'm so happy."*

*"I am just as happy," Papá said. "Seeing how much you and Mateo love each other is a blessing. I know he will take care of you."*

*I desperately tried to blink away my tears before they could fall. I'd promised myself I wouldn't break down. Not yet. Not while there was still time.*

*"Don't cry, Avelina. Even when I am no longer here physically, I will always be with you. Our gift is not time and there is nothing we can do to change that. What we got was quality, which I think is better than quantity. Hold on to the happiest memories while we enjoy every second we have left. You are the light of my life, what has made it worth living..."*

"Are you all right, Miss Saez?"

Jolted from the memory, I turned and looked at the seamstress as I sniffled. Only then did I realize my face was wet. I wiped frantically at the tears on my cheeks.

"I'm sorry," I croaked. "Memories."

She tut-tutted and assured me crying in a wedding

gown was normal before pushing a wad of tissues into my hand.

"The good news is that the fitting is all wrapped up. I'll get you right out of the dress," she said soothingly.

I cleared my throat and nodded. "Of course. I'm so sorry."

"Nothing to apologize for. I'm so used to the brides crying that I keep the tissues close at hand," she assured me as she gestured to a small table against the wall that held bottles of water and two boxes of tissues.

I smiled, grateful for her kindness. She took charge of the conversation, asking me questions about Barcelona as she helped me from the dress.

"I've always wanted to visit," she said. "My husband and I are planning a trip as soon as our youngest graduates high school at the end of next year."

I smiled as I stepped out of the dress and pulled the cotton dress I'd come in over my head. Adjusting it at my hips, I looked over my shoulder at her.

"It's worth the trip," I told her. "It really is the most beautiful place on earth."

She grinned as she finished putting my gown back on its hanger. "We could have gone last year for our twentieth anniversary if that fool hadn't insisted on buying me an Audi. Can you imagine? We live in the city so it isn't as though I get a lot of chances to drive!"

A shiver raced up my spine as my head swiveled back toward the mirror. I reached out to it in order to anchor myself as the edges of my vision blurred and one thought raced through my head—I'd made a huge mistake pushing Mateo away and punishing him for something he didn't do. He wasn't the one who had hurt me.

*"Would you prefer to have lived the remainder of your life with your head in the sand?"*

*"I can't believe you're doing this. How could you?"*

*I raced out to the sidewalk in a huff, clicking unlock on the key fob in my hand as I made my way to the white Audi A7 at the curb. Sliding into the driver's seat, I adjusted it quickly before strapping myself in. I turned the car on and then looked over at the flash drive hanging out of my purse, my stomach rolling as I did. Was it true?*

I heard the seamstress frantically calling out from somewhere close by. "Oh my God! Miss Saez? Miss Saez!"

And then, blessedly, there was nothing.

# Thirteen

I was sitting in the back of a Suburban parked five cars behind the one that had taken Ava to her appointment was parked. I knew it was stalker behavior but did not care one little bit. I needed to be near her, even when she did not know I was there.

A week or so after I followed her to the States, I had my stepmother take charge of having the wedding gown sent along so it could be altered as soon as my runaway bride got her memory back.

*"I will send it, but just so you know, you are not allowed to go with her to the fitting,"* Camila scolded.

*I had been so out of it that her instructions confused me.*

*"Why not?"*

*"Because it's bad luck for the groom to see the dress before the wedding. Traditions like that are important to us girls."*

I wanted nothing more than to escort her to the

appointment this morning, but I knew Camila was right. Tradition was important. Plus, I was doing my best to give Ava space, just like I had promised Alejandro I would.

The day before was a nightmare from start to finish. Keeping my distance from her went against every damn one of my instincts. I forced myself to stay in my office, which had been awful. I had felt a lot like a heroin addict trying desperately to avoid a needle on the other side of the door. The only difference was that in my case, I loved my addiction more than anything in the world. Ava didn't make me weak—she made me strong. Even in the depths of gut-wrenching despair, my love for her was unshakable. Entire cities could be built upon it. I knew of nothing in the world that was stronger than the way I felt about that beautiful, enthralling and stubborn woman.

Movement from the sidewalk ahead caught my attention. Setting my tablet down, I went to look out the windshield at the very same moment the driver turned and looked at me.

His eyes were wide as they met mine. "It's Carlton," he said.

He was right—the movement I was seeing was one of the security team members frantically waving at the car. Flinging the door open, I raced down the sidewalk at high speed.

"What is it? What has happened?" I yelled frantically.

"She's on the floor unconscious—"

"Call 911," I bellowed. Now!"

The panic was so all consuming I felt as if my chest might explode. I barreled past him and yanked the door to the boutique open with such force I heard some of the glass cracking.

"Where is she?"

A woman in a red suit pointed her trembling hand arm toward the back. "The dressing area," she squeaked.

I raced across the room, jumping over a clipboard that had been dropped on the floor. I found where Avelina was easily due to the small crowd of people outside the dressing room. I was so out of my damn mind I did not have it in me to be patient. They sprang back when I yelled for everyone to move the fuck out of my way.

Inside the room the second security guard was on the floor with Ava, waving a cylinder of smelling salts beneath her nose. She was white as a sheet, the ruby color of her lips a sickening contrast to her lack of color. I dropped to the floor beside her and laid my head over her heart, praying to God I wasn't going to lose her. I think I took my first breath since I had sprung out of the car when I heard the thud-thud-thud of her heart beneath my ear.

She jerked her head away from the packet the guard was still waving beneath her nose, which I took as a good sign. Still, she was not opening her eyes and I could not think of a good reason for that.

I looked up and noticed a woman standing against the back wall clutching her necklace nervously.

"What happened?"

"We- she..." swallowing, the woman fanned her face as she got herself under control. "We had just concluded the fitting," she said after a few seconds. "Everything was fine! We were talking about Barcelona and all of a sudden she lost all of her color and fell toward the mirror."

Worst-case scenarios played out in my head. "Did she

hit her head?" I asked.

"No. I grabbed her before she hit the mirror and guided her down to the floor."

"Are you sure? It is very important," I stressed.

"I am one hundred percent sure she didn't hit her head," the woman assured me. "I had one of my hands cradling the base of her skull as I set her down."

Before I could say anything else, an EMT entered the room and told us all to step back. I got to my feet and did as instructed as his partner came in the room.

"This is my fiancée. She suffered a traumatic brain injury a few months ago and has some retrograde amnesia because of it," I informed him frantically.

They sprang into action and asked a dozen questions about what had happened before as well as today. Ava's eyes opened as they were putting her on a spine board. She blinked dazedly before her eyes went wide when she saw me.

"What happened?" she asked.

"You fainted," the first EMT answered.

Ava's eyes stayed on mine. "Am I okay?" she mouthed.

I nodded as they lifted her up and onto a yellow gurney and began checking her vitals, but I could tell she saw the panic in my eyes.

"I'm so sorry, Mateo. Please don't leave me," she whispered.

I did not know if she was apologizing for fainting or for running from me for months, nor did I know whether she meant not to leave her right then or ever. It did not matter since I was going nowhere. My hand went to my heart as I stared down at her.

"Never," I vowed.

"Everything looks fine now, but your fiancé told us you suffered a TBI a few months ago. Out of an abundance of caution, we're going to transport you to the hospital for a full review."

I was surprised when Ava nodded instead of arguing because she hated hospitals.

I walked behind the gurney as they headed for the ambulance, arguing with the EMT's the entire way that I needed to be allowed to ride with her. No matter how I tried, they were not having it—not even when I stooped to an all time low and offered them money.

I would not have stopped trying to find a way around the rules if Ava had not called my name softly.

Grabbing her hand, I leaned over the stretcher. Her coloring was back, but she looked utterly wrecked.

"Just follow behind," she said. "As long as I know you're there, it's fine."

I nodded, turning to tell the guard at my side to have the car brought up. He was already on it, gesturing to the street where the Suburban was already sitting just steps away. In my frantic need to get into the ambulance with her, I had not noticed it pulling up.

"I will be right there," I promised her.

My security was trained in evasive maneuvers and defensive driving, which meant they were more than capable of keeping up with the ambulance. I left them to it but did not take my eyes off the flashing lights ahead of me for one moment. My hands shook as I called Alejandro from the car and brought him up to speed.

"I'll be there in twenty minutes tops," he assured me

before hanging up.

Never before had I been so glad for the universe making certain I found my way to my large family. Without them to hold me up, I was not certain I would still be standing.

# Fourteen

WITH MATEO IN CHARGE, IT DIDN'T TAKE long for the ER staff to transfer me to a private room. I'd have argued with him about the way he went about it, but I was almost as nervous as he was. There had been almost zero warning that I was going to pass out. When my memory loss, mood swings and irritability since the accident were factored in I couldn't completely discount the idea that something deeper might be going on.

Mateo seemed to understand that I needed not to focus on the tension between us without my ever having to say a word. Instead of being on eggshells, we talked to each other normally. Other than when they forced him to, he never left my side. He stayed right there, silently lending me his strength. He kept my hand clasped in his and I never once complained or tried to pull away.

Things become very clear when you think there might be something really wrong with you. In that moment I realized the one thing I was most certain about in this life were my feelings for him. When I was panicking on the floor, it was him I looked for. When they said they were going to transport me to the hospital, it was him I needed. Not anyone else—just Mateo. That said everything. I'd already made up my mind to talk to him about everything that was going on, but I didn't want to do it in the hospital.

Alejandro had been in and out of my room and the entire family called several times as Mateo and I came and went from different tests. Once we got back from radiology and there was nothing to do but sit and wait, Alejandro entertained us with stories about his dating life. I loved Jandro's stories, mostly because I would never have to deal with the craziness of the dating pool. Camila and I teased him often that he had Seinfeld Syndrome—meaning he could find something wrong with any woman.

"You have to have had at least one good date in the last few months," I prodded.

Jandro's blue eyes sparkled as he laughed. "You didn't let me get to the best part," he teased. "One of my college buddies is getting married and his fiancée set me up with one of her co-workers. You know how I feel about blind date shit, but she swore the girl was the complete package. I've been in New York long enough that they weren't taking my excuses anymore, so I gave in and set up the date with Charlotte."

"We met at a restaurant because she worked nearby, which I knew was her get the hell out card in case I was a dog or a dick. No problem there, it was a smart move and one I could totally understand. When Charlotte showed up to the restaurant I was encouraged because Morgan and Robert weren't full of shit. The girl was beautiful and didn't present as a husband-hunter at all. Her skirt went down past her ass, she didn't flash the clam at me even once, her tits weren't on display and she spoke in full – and coherent—sentences. Bonus, she chewed with her mouth closed, she didn't obsessively look at her cellphone *and* she didn't talk in that fake baby doll voice I hate so much."

"She sounds so normal," I said. "Are you going to see her again?"

"Um, hell no," he said dryly. "I'm not done."

"Continue Mr. Seinfeld," I joked.

"Seinfeld could have used this as material. Anyway, dinner was going great and I was feeling good about it so I took her up on her offer to go back to her place. It was a no-brainer, right?"

"Sure," I drawled. "It had all the signs of being a great date. When she invited you to take her home after knowing you for two hours it had to have seemed like a fairytale."

He wiggled his eyebrows suggestively. "Hey, she was looking at all this and couldn't stop herself from wanting it. Who was I to say no?"

I fake gagged and rolled my eyes. "Of course, Alejandro. You're irresistible."

"To the nuttiest women on earth," Mateo scoffed.

I snort-laughed and elbowed him in the side as I nodded my head. "Good one," I chuckled.

"In this case it's true," Jandro conceded. "The second we got through the door to her apartment, I knew I was in trouble. It was a studio apartment, which means it was small and the place was a mess. There were dirty clothes all over the floor, including the hallway galley kitchen where I noticed underwear soaking in the sink. I figured maybe she just had organization issues and gave it a pass. Once I navigated my way through that terror and we got into the main room things took a turn for the worse. Beside the bed—right out for everyone to see—was an industrial sized thing of lube. The thing had a pump and everything. A jug of lube, Ava. *A jug.* Is that something you need to go to Costco for?"

The look on his face was one of complete disbelief and I could tell he really wanted an answer. I was laughing so hard my shoulders were shaking, but I had no idea where one would buy a jug of lube since Mateo and I didn't use it. "I don't know," I choked past my hysterical laughter.

"There was a trashcan next to the bed and, I shit you not, the thing was *full* of wrappers and tied off condoms, and I'm not talking about an itty-bitty trashcan. Either she doesn't empty her garbage for years at a time or she's recently been working her way through Manhattan."

"Cristo, I *really* hope you left," Mateo said.

"Of course I left," Jandro huffed. "Even with a condom there's always a chance shit could go wrong. I'm not trying to get an STD or become an Eskimo brother to all of New York and most of New Jersey."

I laughed so hard I almost cried, and I was happy to see Mateo laughing along with me. Lord knew we needed to smile more. The moment came to an abrupt end when the door to my room opened and the doctor strolled in. Alejandro stood up to beat a hasty retreat, mouthing that he'd be in the hall.

Dr. Bailey immediately put us at ease. The EKG and MRI had both been clear, no abnormalities. All of my vitals were perfect, as was the preliminary blood work. The full blood panel report wouldn't be in until the following day, but since the MRI was fine, the doctor declared that I was good to go home. That was the big relief of the day for me. I hadn't said a word to Mateo, but since the moment I'd awoken on the floor of the dressing room my fear had been that I had the same thing that ultimately killed my father. Although I didn't say it aloud, I knew Mateo could tell. I knew this because it was obvious to me it was his fear as well.

Alejandro came back in once the doctor left the room to finish my discharge paperwork. After we told him the good news I left him and Mateo to talk when I went into the bathroom to change from the hospital gown. I was relieved—beyond, really—to have gotten a clean bill of health. It banked down my nerves and made things very, very clear. I had been given a second chance to get my life back and I wasn't going to let it go. My number one priority was talking things out with Mateo so we could start fresh.

I just hoped I could convince him to forget that one single day of our past.

"Are you hungry?" Mateo asked as we pulled away from the hospital.

I was surprisingly ravenous. "Starving," I admitted.

An expression of surprise flickered across his face.

"Tell me what you want to eat and we will stop to pick it up."

My hunger was no joke, so much so that it was almost all-consuming. After months of not being motivated by food, the fact that I wanted multiple things was a relief. I closed my eyes and tried to narrow down my cravings to one restaurant.

I smiled when I opened my eyes. "Chinese food. Eggrolls, cashew chicken, broccoli beef, fried rice and some hot and sour soup. Oh! Don't forget I like two extra orders of crunchy noodles."

His eyebrows were somewhere up by his hairline. "You really are hungry," he murmured.

"I really am," I assured him.

He reached out and took my hand in his as he leaned forward and told the security guard sitting in the passenger seat where to call and what to order. When he sat back, he let go of my hand and undid his seatbelt before he slid across the seat so he was right next to me. I smiled when he slid his arm across my shoulders. I instinctively curled into him, seeking the warmth only he could provide.

We stayed that way for the remainder of the ride to the Chinese restaurant we favored. After security came back and handed the bag of food off to us, my stomach let out a loud groan. Mateo laughed as he reached into the bag and pulled out a pack of crunchy noodles for me. I tore the bag open and grinned as I popped in a mouthful of the freshly made deliciousness.

"I never thought a stomach growling could make me so happy," Mateo said.

"Me either," I admitted as I tossed a few more into my

mouth. "Oh my God, these noodles are *so* good."

"Yes, they look it," he chuckled.

I elbowed him in the side and laughed before pulling out a few noodles for him. Holding my hand up, I smiled as he leaned down and pulled them into his mouth. His eyes closed as he chewed.

"Mm-hmm," he groaned before he swallowed. "They really are spot on tonight."

"It's probably good we can't get their food in Barcelona because if we could, I'd likely eat it so often I would become an eggroll," I joked.

"While we are in New York it would not be a bad thing for you to eat it every day," he said softly.

I didn't get a chance to respond since the car had pulled into the underground garage. After Mateo helped me from the car he linked his left hand with my right and guided me to the elevator. When the doors opened into the apartment, I felt like I saw it with new eyes. A few days before it had made me anxious to step off the elevator back into this life, but now it felt like coming home, especially since every bit of the décor had been chosen to begin our lives together.

We set ourselves up at the kitchen table and dug in. Mateo was equally as ravenous as I was, the only difference being that he was able to consume more food than I could. As hungry as he was he still took the time to hold his chopsticks out to me again and again with bites of food. I felt myself melting inside at the sweet familiarity of the gesture. From the very beginning, he'd always been my caveman, anxious to make sure I was taken care of before he was. By the time I had finished my final bite, I was teetering on the cusp of being uncomfortably full. I put the leftovers away knowing we'd be back for them at some point and then wiped the table down.

While Mateo dealt with the dishes, I went into the living room and pressed a button to start the scent warmer. As I did, Mateo came up from behind and wrapped his arms around my waist. A whoosh of breath left me as I leaned back against him.

"You scared me today," he said quietly.

The fear in his voice hurt me because I knew I was solely responsible for it. He'd been a rock for me and I'd done nothing but push him away. A lesser man would have thrown in the towel and left without looking back. I was beyond lucky the man I loved wasn't like that because if he had been, I'd have wound up without him for the rest of my life. The very idea made my blood run cold as a shudder ran through me.

I turned in his arms and looked up into his eyes. "I'm so sorry, baby. As horrible as it was, I am glad today happened. It forced me to pull my head out of my ass."

He searched my face before nodding. "This means you remembered," he said.

My eyes darted away as I shook my head in the negative. "Not that day, no. But I did remember what was important and for me, that's always going to be you. Nothing else matters."

He frowned down at me. "So your last memory is still hearing the tape?"

"Not exactly," I hedged. "I did remember getting into the car. It's not important anymore. We're here, now. We can just move on."

He stepped away and dragged his hands through his hair. "Move on with you thinking that what you heard was true?"

I stepped forward, shaking my head frantically. "No," I said emphatically. "I *know* that wasn't true. I'm just saying the rest of it doesn't matter. However I got it, whoever gave it to me, it's over. Whenever I start to recall things from that day I get sick. Today it was so bad I wound up on the floor of a dressing room and spent the next six hours in the hospital because of it. I can't remember because I'm not meant to."

His conflicting thoughts were all over his face. "We should talk to your therapist—"

"No! That's *exactly* what we don't need to do. I found my way back to you, Mateo. You are all that matters. Why do I need to remember? It won't do anything but make me sick. Haven't we lost enough? I can't do it anymore and I'm not going back to therapy. I just want to be with you. Let's put the past behind us."

"I do not think it works that way, mi amor," he sighed.

"Yes it does," I countered firmly. "I don't want to remember so I'm not going to. I've made up my mind."

"Dios, eres hermosa, incluso cuando estás siendo tan terca."

I couldn't help the smile that spread across my face when he said I was beautiful even when I was being stubborn. Stepping in closer, I wound my arms around his torso and tilted my head back.

"You love it when I'm headstrong," I teased.

He reached up and fed his hands into my hair. "I love everything about you," he answered. "What I do *not* love is seeing you in pain."

"Then let me pack it away and move on," I pleaded.

"Ava—"

"Please, Mateo. *Please*."

His throat bobbed as he swallowed thickly. "I just want you to be healthy and happy," he answered.

"I am happy and healthy with you," I assured him. "Give me a chance to move beyond all of this. It's all I need."

His eyes fluttered shut as he nodded his head once before opening them. "We will try it your way for now," he sighed.

The last bit of anxiety I'd been holding onto melted away, which only left me in need of one thing to feel perfect. I leaned in closer and unlinked my hands from around his torso so I could slide them down to his perfect ass.

"Bésame," I whispered.

I didn't need to ask twice. His head came down fast, covering my lips with his. It was like taking a breath of air after being submerged for far too long. There was no middle ground in the kiss. Although the tenderness of the love we shared was ever present, the need to connect made us frantic. His hands held my head in place as he plundered my mouth, dominating me with the smooth strokes of his tongue.

Desperate to feel his skin, I yanked his shirt from his pants. The buttons were nothing but an impediment, one I couldn't tolerate. Without care, I ripped the shirt apart from the bottom up as he continued to devour my mouth. It wasn't just me who was frantic. The way he groaned when I slid my hands up his abs made my core clench like crazy.

Any semblance of control was lost. Ripping my mouth from his, I dropped to my knees on the living room floor. His breath came in rapid gusts as I undid his belt and the top button of his pants before sliding the zipper down. I looked up and met his gaze as his pants dropped to his ankles. Not giving him a chance to take off his shoes and kick the pants off, I reached into his boxer briefs and to his shaft into my fist. Licking my lips, I pulled it out. The tip was wet with pre-cum, and I smiled before I stuck out my tongue and wiggled it against the head.

"God, Avelina…"

I stared into his eyes as I opened my mouth and sucked him inside and hollowed out my cheeks the way I knew drove him insane.

His hands gripped my head firmly as he guided himself back and forth in my mouth, his eyes asking for permission to take the next step. I relaxed my throat and nodded before letting out a moan as he thrust in deep, the tip of him hitting the back of my throat. I loved watching the last vestiges of his control slip away as he worked himself in and out. Unable to help myself I yanked up my dress and slid my fingers beneath the elastic of my soaked underwear.

"Mi amor," he groaned when he realized what I was doing, his voice guttural and thick with desire.

I hummed around his length as I rubbed two fingers against my clit. My movements quickened as he thrust harder and faster into my mouth. I could tell by the look in his eyes that he was holding on by a thread and I didn't intend to come without him inside of me. It had been too long and I needed it too much. I pulled my fingers out from my underwear and tapped on his thigh, which was our agreed on signal for him to stop. He groaned as his hands let go of my head and he popped out of my mouth.

"Get down here," I panted.

He nodded as he dropped to his knees on the floor in front of me. I set a hand on his chest and pushed back gently.

"On your back."

How he did it with his pants still around his ankles, I'll never know. Somehow, he managed it. I had straddled him before he was in that position for even a second. With my dress shoved up around my thighs, I pushed my underwear to the side with my left hand as I rose up over him and gripped his shaft with my right. His back arched off the floor as I pushed down on him, the fit so damn tight I could barely breathe.

Any other time I would have savored a slow descent, but I couldn't wait. Bracing my hands on his chest, I rose up and then sank down hard, impaling myself on the entire length of his shaft.

"Cristo," he bellowed, his voice ringing throughout the penthouse.

I cried out my agreement as I rocked back and forth on him frantically, my nails digging into the skin of his chest as I did. We were reduced to grunting, groaning and begging for more, harder, and faster. He held my hips as I leaned over and kissed him while he thrust up into me desperately. With the tip of his shaft hitting the special spot inside of me that made me wild, I knew I wasn't going to be able to take much more. I tore my mouth from his and let out a screech as he bounced me on top of him and fucked me harder.

"More," I begged.

He pounded up into me harder, grunting as he did. "Como te sientes. Tan buena. Tan apretada. Me voy a venir" he groaned.

That was what I'd been looking for—the moment he said he wanted to come I started to go over. I had never wanted to feel the heat of his release inside of me more than I did in that moment. I didn't just want it—I craved it. My head fell back as my orgasm lit me up from the inside out, leaving me breathless as he fucked me through it.

I thought he'd come right then, but he didn't. As I writhed on top of him he rolled us over so I was on my back. With his hands supporting him on either side of my head, he pounded into me with punishing thrusts. I wrapped my legs around his waist and gripped onto his back as I continued to come, my orgasm now a living, breathing thing that refused to be stopped.

"Mateo," I screamed as he fucked harder.

"Vente sobre mi polla," he growled, telling me to come around his dick.

I couldn't have stopped if I wanted to, and I didn't. One orgasm bled into another like a storm touching down on the sea. Tears poured from my eyes as I stared up at him, the release so profound it felt like it was tearing down everything inside of me so I could be built anew.

"I love you, I love you, I love you, I love you," I cried as he thrust deep, rooting himself so far inside I felt him in every part of me. I held him tighter and loved him harder when I realized he was crying, too.

"Let go," I whimpered. "I've got you, baby. Just let go."

"Te amo, te amo, siempre Ava, te amo siempre te amare," he rasped.

His body began to shake as his thrusts grew frantic and his tears fell, blending with my own on my cheeks. He yelled my name again as his shaft jerked inside of me and I felt the first jet of his release. It went on and on as he gasped and growled on top of me, the only coherent word from his mouth was my name.

When it was over, he collapsed on top of me and buried his face in my neck, his body trembling from the force of our union. I loved the sensation of his hot breath against my sensitive skin. I kept my legs around his waist and ran my fingers through his hair as he came back to himself.

"Hold onto me," he instructed.

I knew what he wanted so I complied without question, smiling as he rolled onto his back. I snuggled against his chest and breathed in the heady smell of him. As hard as he'd come, he wasn't fully soft inside of me. His hands cupped my buttock as he held me close.

I lifted my head so I could touch his face, my lips kissing along the tracks of his tears. "I love you so much," I told him over and over again.

"I love you just as much," he answered.

I kissed his lips softly before setting my head back down on his chest. I never wanted to get up off the floor.

"I have lived for this moment," he sighed. "The only thing that kept me going was faith that someday I would be able to hold you again."

"I'm so sorry," I sniffled against his chest.

He ran his hands up my back gently as he shushed me.

"Do not apologize for the situation you did not create," he said firmly. "Nothing can or will ever keep us apart again. I will not allow it. No matter what life throws at us in the future, we will face it together."

I swallowed past the lump in my throat and smiled at his words. Whenever there was a crisis Mateo was always by my side with those same words on facing all of life's challenges together.

I hoped things would calm down enough that he wouldn't have to say them again anytime soon.

# Fifteen

*Ava—the past*

I YAWNED AND SNUGGLED IN CLOSER TO MATEO'S chest, trailing my foot up his shin as I did so. I was so happy to have him in my time zone I could barely contain my joy. Upon his arrival back from New York, we had spent one night in Barcelona in my father's guesthouse before Mateo whisked me off to Cullera Beach, the area of Valencia he'd been raised in.

Since then we'd spent three days and three nights in the villa he'd rented for us. It overlooked the sea and had a beautiful pool, but other than eating and bathing, we hadn't really left the bedroom. After not seeing him the two months prior, I wasn't complaining one little bit. We were insatiable for each other and there wasn't a thing wrong with that.

I tickled his calf with my foot again, trying to wake him up. On my fourth attempt, he chuckled and ran his right hand up my side.

"I love waking up with you," he murmured, his voice

still thick with sleep.

"That's good since you get to do it every day now," I murmured. "I'm so glad you were able to negotiate leaving New York early. Another seven months of being apart the majority of the time might've killed me."

"It definitely would have killed me," he chuckled. "Never again will we be separated. It was like being separated from a limb. Wherever you are, I will be."

I nuzzled against his chest and smiled.

"I love that answer."

"And I love you," he replied.

Declarations of love quickly led to kissing which inevitably led to touching and soon after we were busy burning up the sheets. I knew that once again we wouldn't be leaving the bed to explore Valencia that day and I didn't care one bit.

I hummed to myself as I worked through the last of my math work at the table in my father's kitchen. Over the course of the past year and a half, Mateo and I had settled into a routine that suited us both perfectly. We alternated our time between an apartment he'd purchased in Barcelona near work and the guesthouse of my father's villa. It was unconventional, but Papá had firmly told us we would not be living together full time until we were married. Since Mateo and I never slept apart, it was no more than a technicality, really. Everyone knew we were going to get married as soon as I graduated from college, but until then, living together was perfect—even with my father demanding that we not officially live in the

Barcelona apartment together.

The great thing was that the edict worked for Mateo and me as a couple. I enjoyed being able to see my father several days a week and it also meant Mateo's relationship with his own father grew that much closer since they were neighbors. We hadn't yet told our parents but our long-term plan was to purchase a home within their gated enclave. I'd always loved it and Mateo thought it was the perfect place to raise our children.

As joyfully as I anticipated our future, most days I was so focused our amazing present that I just reveled in that. A noise from the driveway pulled me from my work. Pushing the calculator aside, I looked toward the back door. I smiled as it opened and I saw my father entering with two members of his security team just behind him.

"You're home early," I noted.

As he came closer, I realized his coloring was terrible. Jumping up, I raced to his side.

"What's wrong Papá?"

"I have a terrible headache," he admitted.

I noticed he was unsteady on his feet at the moment his security team stepped forward to flank him on either side so he wouldn't fall over.

"Your heart?"

"No," he whispered. "That is fine. This is my head."

The security team guided him into the sitting room and helped him sit down. He leaned back and covered his eyes with a trembling hand.

I looked to Pascal, the lead security guard. "How long has this been going on?"

"He's been getting a lot of headaches for the last two

or three months, but this is the biggest yet."

"Then why didn't he go to the doctor instead of coming home?" I asked frantically.

"You know your father, Avelina. He refused," Pascal replied. "He wanted to be home."

I shook my head just as my father made a noise of distress that made my blood run cold. I dropped onto the sofa next to him and clutched his hand.

"Papá?"

He opened his mouth like he was going to answer, but nothing came out. Instead, his entire body went completely stiff and began shaking. When it was over, he was unconscious.

The second security guard called for an ambulance as I cried frantically and tried to wake my father up.

Camila appeared shortly after the ambulance pulled in, the sound of the siren having alerted her to the problem. She stayed with me as we were hustled into the back of the car and driven behind the ambulance to the hospital and then took control of calling Mateo, handing the phone off to me after she'd given him the details.

I knew right away that he was leaving the office because I could hear him moving swiftly. "I am going down to my car now. I will be at the hospital as soon as humanly possible," he assured me. "Stay strong, mi tesoro. I will be with you shortly."

I was crying too hard to do more than tell him the most important thing. "I love you."

"I love you more," he answered.

My father was in the hospital for three days before we got any answers. An MRI, a brain scan, blood tests and God only knew what other tests had been run. During the first day all they could give him for the pain was morphine, so he was pretty out of it as test after test was run. The second day he seemed to feel a bit better, but admitted he was exhausted.

Toward the end of the third day, Antonio, Mateo and I were seated in chairs by the side of his bed when the doctor came in and gave the diagnosis. Papá was awake and alert, which I hoped was a good sign. I was doing my best to stay positive, but for a fraction of a second when the door opened for the doctor to enter, I could see on his face that he didn't think the news would be good.

"I'm sorry to tell you that you have an inoperable brain tumor," Dr. Savitz said to my father.

I'd been holding onto my father's right hand as the doctor made the announcement. Papá squeezed my fingers at the same time Mateo began running his hand up and down my back soothingly. Only then did I realize I'd made a sound of distress. I swallowed past the lump in my throat as I patted my father's arm.

"I'm okay."

I knew he could tell I was lying, but there wasn't anything to be done for it. When someone hands down a diagnosis like that, it isn't something you can shrug off. Those three words—inoperable brain tumor—rocked my world off its axis.

"What makes it inoperable?" Papá questioned.

"What you have is called astrocytomas glioblastoma. It is in your brain stem, an area that we can't operate on.

Unfortunately, your tests have also shown that the cancer is spreading. There are two pea-sized tumors in your right lung and another slightly larger one in your left."

"How long?" my father asked.

"There are things we can do to slow it down, but even with that you're looking at about a year."

My chest felt like the weight of an entire building had collapsed down on me, the agony so acute I thought it might pull me under. "A year?" I croaked.

A year wasn't enough time. Twenty years wouldn't be enough time. I needed my father!

"I'm very, very sorry," Dr. Savitz answered. "I know this is the worst possible news."

"There must be something we can do," Antonio said. "Another opinion? Experimental treatments? Money is no object. There has to be *something*!"

The doctor shook his head. "I sent the test results to a doctor at the Mayo Clinic last night and consulted with two more of my stateside peers this morning. There is nothing that will cure this."

It was at that moment I realized one of the things my father had stressed to me my entire life was one hundred percent true. There were many things in life that were unchangeable, no matter how much money you had. It was why he'd been so passionate about teaching me to live with compassion and honor—because you never knew when your time would be up.

Money could never make you a good person—only your actions did that. I'd always known I'd learned more important things from my father than I ever had from my mother, but never was it more apparent to me than it was right then. If I'd taken after her, I'd have been stomping my feet and threatening lawsuits because it all came down to money with her. I knew it was petty but I couldn't help the moment of relief I experienced when I realized I wouldn't have to talk to her about what was going on with Papá. She would only have said something to upset me more than I already was.

The conversation with Dr. Savitz lasted almost a full hour. He took his time and explained everything—often twice—so that we all got the full gist. The long-term picture was awful, the absolute worst thing I could ever have imagined.

Two things kept me from falling to the floor. The first was my need not to upset my father. The second was Mateo's firm grasp on me. Talk about treatment options went over my head, mostly because I was so overwhelmed the diagnosis that I couldn't wrap my mind around anything else. I'm not sure how my father kept himself together. Maybe it was the shock of it, or maybe it was that he'd sensed something was really wrong all along.

After Dr. Savitz had left, the room was silent for countless seconds. It was my father who spoke first.

"We have two choices here. Either we spend the next few months crying and waiting for the end, losing the time we have left being depressed, or we take the advanced notice as the gift it is and make the best of the time I have left."

"Only you would find something positive to say right now," Antonio said, his voice cracking with emotion.

As heartbreaking as that moment was my father's smile lit up his entire face. "I have had a blessed life," he answered. "I had true love with a beautiful wife I loved with my whole heart. Losing her taught me the most important lesson of all—time is not promised. After Valeria had died, I believed I would never find true happiness again, but I was wrong. My life began anew when I was gifted with a beautiful and amazing child who has made every single day since her birth a dream. I have an amazing best friend who provided me with five amazing nephews that I love and adore. We built a business from the ground up that succeeded beyond our wildest dreams. After my heart attack, I was given yet another chance. All of the time since then has been a bonus."

My eyes were wet with tears as I clutched his hand like a lifeline.

"Papá," I sobbed.

"Don't cry just yet, mi ángel. I am still here. We will enjoy the time we have left and leave nothing unsaid. Help me go out on a high note."

I nodded as I lifted one of my hands away from his and swiped at the twin tears on my cheeks. For my entire life, my father had been strong for me. Now, it was my turn to be his rock.

# Sixteen

*Ava—Last Year*

A LOT CHANGED OVER THE NEXT WEEK. MATEO and I immediately moved into the guesthouse at my father's villa full time. I'd also taken a leave of absence from school. I'd thought everyone would fight me on it, but no one did. My intent was to spend as much time as humanly possible with my father, and school didn't fit into that plan. I had a lifetime ahead of me to finish college—but only a short amount of time left to spend with Papá.

Mateo and I were set to take him to his first radio-therapy appointment in the morning. Tonight, Papá had asked for the two of us to sit down with him and Antonio after dinner. I was nervous about the meeting because I had a horrible suspicion it was going to involve his will, something I didn't want to talk about at all.

Two days after he was released from the hospital he had his living will updated so his final wishes were clear. I was barely able to hold myself together when he made it clear that he did not want to be kept alive by machines.

*"Until there is nothing left for me to do, I will fight this thing. But, when the day comes that my body gives out and I go down, let me go with a clear conscience and no guilt. You must know that you are following through on what my choice is, one I am making while I am still able to do so. I do not want to be resuscitated,"* he said.

Every bit of it hurt, like pieces of my soul being slashed at with a hatchet. He wasn't quitting, but he'd also accepted his fate in the calm way he had always had about him. I understood his end was coming—that it was inevitable—but that didn't make it any easier at all.

Mateo held my hand in his as we walked into the informal sitting room off of Papá's office. Already he and Antonio were seated in their big leather seats, puffing away on cigars. They didn't smoke often—maybe a dozen times a year or so. I'd always enjoyed the aromatic and rich aroma of the Cuban cigars they favored, but since Camila hated it, their shared humidor was kept in my father's sitting room.

"I leave you alone for a few hours and you get up to no good," I teased.

Papa's eyes danced as he threw back his head and laughed. "I am caught," he joked.

I let go of Mateo's hand and went to my father, leaning over to drop a kiss on his cheek.

"I'm sure Dr. Savitz would advise against smoking," I noted.

"You'd be wrong," Papá answered. "I asked and he said since I do it so infrequently, it's not like it will make any difference. Don't worry, mi ángel. It will not make me any sicker."

Mateo set his hands on my shoulders, rubbing them softly like he knew I needed his touch. Every mention of my father's health made me tense up.

"So what's this meeting about?" I asked as Mateo guided me to the leather loveseat across from our father's.

Antonio and Papá exchanged a look I imagined they'd first perfected in grade school fifty years before. They'd been friends for so long that it often seemed as if they could read each other's minds.

"I know what I am about to request means changing your plans, but it is something I feel strongly about."

I squeezed Mateo's hand in mine as my heartbeat sped up. My only current plan was to take care of my father. If he was about to say he didn't want me to, I would be crushed.

"Okay," I said slowly.

"I am leaving you in good hands with Mateo, which eases much of my anxiety about passing on. More than a year ago he came and asked for your hand in marriage."

My eyebrows went up in surprise. Mateo and I frequently talked about our future—including when we would marry—but I hadn't known he'd already formally asked my father.

"At that time I agreed," Papá continued, "but asked him to wait for you to graduate college. He told me that you two were already thinking along those lines and that was that. However, in light of what's happening now, I would very much love for you to move it up. Before I go, I would like to see my only daughter become an official part of my best friend's family."

Mateo started nodding before my father had finished the sentence. "Waiting to ask turned out to be even harder than I had anticipated," he murmured.

With a squeeze of my hand, he turned my way. "Is it okay to move our plans up, mi tesoro?"

"Of course! Yes. Let's do this."

He kissed me softly before pulling back to smile at me.

"I would marry you tomorrow," he whispered.

I lit up inside, my answering smile so big it's a wonder it didn't hurt my cheeks. "Any place, anytime," I whispered back.

For those few seconds, we were alone in the world. So much so that I startled when my father spoke again.

"Since the day I put your veil on for your first holy communion, I dreamt about seeing you in your wedding gown. I don't want to miss shopping for it," Papá said, his voice thick with emotion.

Seeing how relieved and happy he was made my heart feel full to bursting.

"I will set up an appointment for us to go dress hunting as soon as possible," I promised.

Antonio clapped my father on the back before he leaned forward and pressed the call button on the house intercom sitting between him and my father.

"It's a done deal. Bring in the champagne," he said happily.

Camila entered the room a minute later with a bottle of champagne clutched in her hand. The glasses were carried by one of the security guards who set them on the coffee table in front of us before exiting the room.

"I told you two old fools there was nothing to be worried about," she teased.

A few minutes later we were toasting to the soon-to-be official merging of the Cruz and Saez families.

That weekend Mateo whisked me away to the city for a getaway the day before I was scheduled to go wedding gown shopping. We checked into the Ritz-Carlton Arts Hotel and had a light lunch before he sent me up to the spa. I spent the next few hours having a diamond dust body massage and facial, followed by a manicure and pedicure. By the time I got back to our suite overlooking the Mediterranean Sea I was so relaxed I felt limp. After kicking off my flip-flops, I fell onto the couch next to Mateo with a sigh of pure happiness as I propped my feet up on the coffee table.

He wrapped his arm around me and pulled me in close as I dropped my head against his chest. "I can't even tell you how absolutely amazing that was," I murmured. "I feel like a new woman."

Mateo ran his hand up and down my arm soothingly and I relaxed further into him. "You are tired," he noted.

I made an hmm sound before nodding. "I don't know if it's that I'm tired, or that I'm just so relaxed that sleep sounds amazing."

"Then we will now enjoy an afternoon siesta," he laughed as he rose from the couch in one fluid movement before bending down and lifting me up.

I grinned like an idiot as he set me down on the floor next to the bed and proceeded to pull off my loose top, my bra and the yoga pants I was wearing within seconds. After divesting himself of everything he was wearing other than his boxer briefs, he lifted me up again and put me into bed before climbing in next to me and pulling me into his arms. I think I fell asleep in under twenty seconds.

Hours later I woke up to Mateo nibbling gently on the side of my neck. Rolling onto my back, I threaded my fingers through his hair and sighed as he followed me, settling between my thighs while his lips began working their way down my neck.

"It is time to wake up, mi tesoro. We need to be downstairs for dinner in just over ninety minutes."

I shifted beneath him and wrapped my legs around his waist, the rigid length of his shaft hot between my legs. "You know I can be ready in less than an hour," I murmured. "I get the feeling you woke me up a little early for something else."

"You caught me," he replied with a low chuckle. "I thought maybe we could take a nice long shower."

"As usual you're full of good ideas," I teased as I rubbed against his hardened length. "But as good as it is, I'm thinking maybe we start here and then clean up in the shower."

He groaned as he ground down against me. "Good idea."

"You are glowing," Mateo growled into my ear as we stepped into the elevator.

I laughed as I leaned into him. "Turns out the diamond dust facial and massage turns into something magical when you follow it up with a siesta and some pre-dinner lovemaking."

We left the elevator hand-in-hand and walked into Enoteca, which was one of my favorite restaurants in Barcelona. My brows went up when I noticed there were no other diners around.

The maître d' nodded when he saw us approaching. "Mr. Cruz, Miss Saez. It is a pleasure to have you with us this evening. Let me show you to your table."

We followed along behind him to our favorite table in the corner—the one I jokingly called ours. As usual, we chose to be seated next to—as opposed to across from— each other. We weren't in our seats for more than a few seconds before the sommelier appeared with a bottle of our favorite *Dominio de Pingus* wine. He poured a bit for Mateo to sniff and taste for approval. Once he had, he poured us both glasses and then left the table.

I leaned in close to whisper to Mateo. "Why are we the only people here?" I asked.

He dropped a swift kiss on my lips before pulling back to smile at me tenderly. "Because I made it so."

His romantic gestures were always something to behold, but this one was even bigger than usual.

"You bought out Enoteca for the night?"

He shrugged as though it were nothing when really it was everything. "I wanted alone time with you."

I reached up and traced my thumb along his lower lip as I wiggled my eyebrows suggestively. "You are getting so lucky later," I vowed.

He captured my thumb between his teeth and smiled at me devilishly before letting it go with a quick kiss.

"I will hold you to that," he teased.

Enoteca's tasting menu was a thing of beauty. One small course after another was served with flair. Over the course of the next two hours, we dined on Thai broth, risotto, lamb, egg benedict, pickled tuna, carrot gnocchi and an absolutely divine grouper. We followed it up with some petit fours before leaving the restaurant fully replete and very happy.

I snuggled against Mateo's chest as we rode the elevator to our floor. When we got to our room he opened the door before grabbing my hand and pulling me down the hallway to the living room. My breath left me when I saw that most of the furniture had been cleared out. Thousands of rose petals were scattered across the floor and dozens of candles flickered around the room, giving the space a soft and romantic glow. In front of me, a photographer was taking photos while another was recording. In the back corner, a string quartet began playing a beautiful piece of music. When I turned to look at the musicians, I realized that there were other far more important to me people gathered in the room as well.

My father, Antonio, Camila and all of Mateo's brothers were right there, even Joaquin who we saw less of than we would have liked now that he was officially a member of Real Madrid. The entire family was there for us, all of them beaming as I took it all in. I was shaking as I turned back to Mateo, my heart lodged somewhere in my throat as the reality of what he was doing hit me.

He grazed my lips with a soft kiss and whispered *te amo, mi amor* before dropping to one knee. Pulling a velvet ring box from his pocket, he popped it open and held it up for me to see. I raised both hands to my lips and gasped when I saw the beautiful emerald and diamond engagement ring glittering up at me. Set in platinum, it was the most gorgeous piece of jewelry I'd ever seen in my life.

"Avelina Marie Saez," he said huskily, "will you spend all the days of this life and any that may follow with me?"

I could feel the tears pouring down my cheeks as I nodded like a bobble-head. "Yes! Yes, yes, yes. Always and forever, yes!" I cried.

"Then give me your hand so we can make this official, mi bello amor."

My hand was shaking as I held it out to him so he could slide the ring—a perfect fit—on to my finger. For those few seconds, I forgot about everyone else in the room because I only saw him. I wasn't even looking at the ring in that moment because I was busy staring at him, committing the moment to memory.

He rose from the floor with masculine grace and pulled me into his arms. I hugged him tight as he wiped away my tears and kissed me over and over again. After all of my tears had been taken care of, he kissed me deeply, dipping me backward as our families applauded. When he brought me back up straight I was almost dizzy from joy.

Papá got to me first, pulling me into his arms and rocking me back and forth as he told me how happy he was to see me so loved. While he hugged me, Alejandro and Joaquin were busy pulling Mateo away to congratulate him. I smiled at them before turning my attention back to my father.

"I can't believe he did this," I said, my voice thick with emotion.

"Of course he did," Papá laughed. "That boy loves you more than anything."

I nodded, sniffling as I swallowed past the lump in my throat.

"I guess I'm just surprised he managed to do all of this and get an engagement ring in the matter of a few days."

My father guffawed as though I'd said something hilarious. "All he had to do was pick the restaurant, sweetie. He's had the ring since before he asked me for my blessing a year ago."

I was stunned. "Are you sure?" I asked.

Papá nodded. "Of course. I saw it with my own two eyes. I was impressed—but not surprised—that he instinctively knew you would want the emerald as opposed to a diamond. The boy has good taste."

I shivered when Mateo wrapped his arms around my waist from behind. "If you are talking about me, I agree wholeheartedly. My good taste led me to Ava, after all."

I smiled as I leaned back against him. "Were your ears burning?" I teased.

He laughed and hugged me tighter. "I believe they were."

We spent the next hour walking around the room hand in hand, mingling with our family in between the toasts our fathers gave and the photos we posed for. I don't think my smile left my face for even a minute of that time.

# Seventeen

*Ava—Present*

AFTER THE NIGHT IN THE LIVING ROOM, WE SPENT the next five days locked in the apartment. Naked. We both heeded the almost endless need to connect, coming together again and again without hesitation. Honestly, I was somewhat surprised either of us could still move. It was obvious both of us were intent on making up for lost time. We took breaks to eat, shower and sleep—but even those times frequently concluded with us making love.

We were out in the pool—which, thankfully, we were able to swim naked in due to a retractable extension from the roof that covered the pool and the patio. It was something Mateo had added on after the first summer we'd gotten together. It was worth every penny and then some. Side by side on our giant raft we held hands as we relaxed, the soothing sound of the waterfalls on either end of the pool lulling me into a trance-like state.

"Have I worn you out?" he asked teasingly.

I kept my eyes closed as I smiled dreamily. "Worn out? No. Replete? Yes. I'm just enjoying being next to you."

He chuckled as his fingers squeezed mine. "I was enjoying the same thing until about two minutes ago."

I cracked an eye and turned to look at him. "What happened two minutes ago?"

He sighed heavily, like something weighed heavily on his mind. "I am surprised you do not know."

"Know what?" I squeaked.

He cracked, his lips quirking a second before he laughed. "It has been almost *three hours* since I have been inside of you," he teased. "I believe that is a record for the last five days."

"Ah," I nodded before letting out a laugh of my own. "Are you saying you would like to change that before we hit hour four?"

"I am feeling very needy," he admitted.

I rolled on to my side and kissed his shoulder affectionately. He smiled at me as I traced my hand down his chest to his abdomen. "Needy?" I questioned as I continued down to his shaft where I ran my thumb over the tip.

His eyes flared as he inhaled sharply.

"Very much so," he said huskily.

"Right here in the pool?" I asked.

"Sí," he growled low in his throat as he moved my hand aside and climbed on top of me.

The raft was enormous, but still it rocked beneath us, churning the water around as he settled between my thighs. Just that quickly, the smoldering fire inside of me lit back up. We were on a hair-trigger, our need for one another right at the surface at all times. I bit my lip as I wrapped my legs around him, setting my feet on the back of his calves.

Mateo leaned in close and rubbed his nose against mine. "I will never get enough of you," he said.

I nodded as I ran my hands up and down his arms and shoulders. "I feel the same," I admitted. "It's never enough."

He grinned wickedly before bending his head and licking along my clavicle. I arched a bit beneath him, loving the way he paid attention to every part of me. As always, the touch of his tongue to my skin and the scent of him, always stronger when he was aroused, set me off. It took that little to turn me on.

"Mateo," I sighed, my hands sliding up from his arms to his shoulders and then up his neck and into his hair.

"Mi tesoro," he answered. "Only you and only *ever* you, Ava. Without you, I am nothing. You are more important to me than anything else in this world."

His love and devotion humbled me, especially in the aftermath of all I'd put him through. Instead of hating me, he loved me more, telling me again and again how much he loved me. I didn't know what I had done to deserve a love like his, but I promised him that I would be the woman he deserved. Each time I said as much he would shut me down.

*"You have always been perfect to me, Avelina. Nothing has changed because there is no way it could. I love you."*

I'd thought I understood that before, but looking back I wonder if there had always been a part of me that feared something would change. Now I didn't just believe, I knew. It was not a guess or a hope—it was a fact.

"I love you," I sighed, smiling as he pulled the lobe of

my ear into his mouth gently.

When he pulled back, I felt his breath against the side of my face. "Take me inside of you," he whispered against my ear. "Bring me home."

Reaching between us, I guided the tip of his shaft to my opening and rubbed it against my arousal.

"Is this what you want?" I teased breathlessly.

"Dios, sí."

My neck arched as I let out a little moan and held him against me. "Take me."

He groaned against my neck as he slowly pushed inside. When he was all the way in, I had to remind myself to breathe as I squeezed around him with my internal muscles. Bringing my feet up from his calves, I linked them behind his lower back.

"You feel so good," he rasped.

We stayed like that, chest to chest, every part of us touching as we refrained from moving, at least until he slipped his hand between us and began swirling his fingers over my clit.

So slowly it was almost too much to bear, he began to slide in and out. The raft rocked on top of the water like a giant waterbed we didn't want to displace.

"Avelina," he whispered as he raised his head from my neck and looked between us. "You look so good when you are full of me."

My inner muscles clenched again, a rolling wave of ecstasy as I watched him watching our joining.

"Mateo," I breathed.

"Mi amor," he replied, just before his lips covered my own.

The kiss was heartbreakingly slow and deep, a connection on some other level that we both seemed to understand we needed right then. His hips continued the in and out movements, purposeful and deliberately bringing me closer to the release I knew only he could provide. I clutched his face between my hands, running my fingers through his sexy stubble as we kissed.

My orgasm washed over me like a rolling wave, powerful but quiet, packing a punch with little fanfare. I tore my lips from his and bit his lower lip, sucking it into my mouth as I came.

"Dios, Ava, te sientes tan bien," he groaned as his shaft jerked and began spilling his hot cum inside of me.

I tilted my head back and watched his face as he came, his eyes opening and holding my own as he let me see everything he was feeling. I doubted anyone had or would ever feel as loved as I was by him. As he finished, I wrapped my arms around his shoulders and pulled him down on top of me, enjoying the serenity that followed on the heels of our lovemaking.

"I love you," I said, my voice strong and clear. "I will *always* love you."

He kissed my neck and told me he loved me more than life itself before pulling out and flopping onto his back next to me on the raft.

He turned his head to look at me and smiled. "That was incredible," he said.

"Not a bad effort, Mr. Cruz," I joked.

"You are so dirty," he laughed. "You are comparing it to our last pool session when I took you from behind and had to cover your mouth so no one heard your cries of pleasure. That was quite a night."

That fast, I couldn't breathe. The pool incident he was talking about had happened the night before my accident. Unable to control my reaction I sat up fast, the raft rocking unsteadily.

Mateo sat up just as fast, his voice frantic as he reached for me.

"Ava! What is it?"

No, no, no. Not now, not now!

I flailed frantically as I tried to push myself off the raft. As I launched into the water, I heard him yelling my name. Seconds later, he was pulling me out of the water, his face taut with panic.

"Talk to me," he demanded. "Look at me, Ava. Look at me!"

I couldn't even breathe because I'd remembered *everything*.

# Eighteen

*Ava—the past*

"I'M VERY SORRY FOR YOUR LOSS."

I nodded and said an automatic thank you, barely aware of who had said the words. I was numb, completely overwhelmed and wrung out. I'd believed I would have a year with my father before he passed. In the end, we only got four months. My wedding had been set for next weekend, but that had been canceled in the face of my father's passing ten days ago. He'd gone quickly and without warning—passing away in his office at work while sitting at his desk. Antonio had gone in to remind him to get ready for his thrice-weekly appointment with Dr. Savitz, only to find that he was already gone.

People said I should feel grateful that his passing had been quick—happening before his pain level was unmanageable—but I didn't have it in me to be positive. I'd been cheated of eight months, and I was angry about it. There would be no more days spent together in the villa's library, no more late lunches on the porch, and, worst of all, no memories of him walking me down the aisle. I was completely gutted, barely able to put one foot in front of the other. The only parent I'd ever been able to rely on was gone and it hurt like nothing I'd ever felt before. Without my father, I felt like an orphan.

The visitation at the church lasted for almost five hours, more than seven hundred people making their way to the front to see my father's urn and offer condolences to me, Mateo, Antonio, Camila and the rest of the Cruz boys. I was flanked between Mateo and Antonio, both who were doing their best to hold me up and keep me going. More than ever, I found myself leaning into Mateo, almost like I hoped I'd be able to soak in some of his strength by osmosis.

When it was all over, and only the family was left in the church, I allowed Mateo to lead me to a pew. I dropped down and let out a long exhale, relieved that the hardest part was behind me. I'd had serious anxiety about the funeral because I'd known the sheer amount of people who were coming would be overwhelming to me emotionally.

Mateo took a seat next to me, wrapping his arm around my shoulders as he pulled me into him.

"It is done," he said.

I nodded, my eyes on the urn that sat on the altar. If things had gone the way they were meant to, we would be getting the final things ready for the wedding and next week we'd be standing in front of that altar getting married. I blamed myself for agreeing with my father when he'd insisted he wanted me to have a huge wedding. The sheer size of it made it impossible to plan quickly. Even throwing money at the situation couldn't change the logistics of a wedding being attended by six hundred people. I hated myself for not forcing the issue. If I had, he'd have been alive to walk me down the aisle. Now, that could never happen.

Almost as painful as losing my father was the way Antonio seemed to age a decade overnight. It broke my heart to see how losing his best friend completely destroyed him. I believed he would recover, but his grief was a mirror for my own. They had been best friends since kindergarten fifty-five years ago. I understood the scope of the loss, even though I wished I'd been blessed by fifty-five years with my father as opposed to the twenty-one I'd had.

I stood as Antonio came forward with his arms open. I fell into them, sniffling against his shirt as I cried. I realized he was crying too when I felt his chest shaking with great heaving sobs beneath my cheek. We stayed that way for countless minutes, holding on to each other silently as we both sobbed. At some point I took a tissue that was handed to me, using it to mop up the flood of tears on my cheeks. When we separated, I was completely wrung out.

"I need to tell you something," Antonio said, his voice choked with emotion.

Mateo handed me another tissue, and I used it to blow my nose as I nodded.

"Okay," I said slowly, fearing whatever he had to say would be bad. I didn't know how much more I could take.

"Quino made me promise that after he was gone and the funeral was over, I'd convince you to go away for a bit. He wanted you to have time away from the villa while you mourned."

I sniffled and wiped at my nose, not understanding how a change in my surroundings could possibly make anything different. My father was dead. Nothing would make that hurt less.

"Why?"

"He hoped that you and Mateo would make the villa your permanent residence. Because of this, he believed it was important that you not associate it as a place of mourning. That house has always brought you joy—he wanted to keep it that way."

Mateo kneaded my shoulders gently, a silent reminder that he had my back and would be there, whatever I decided.

"I… I don't know that I'd feel right leaving," I hedged. "The will was only just read. Don't I have to do anything?"

Antonio shook his head. "It was a simple will, really. Other than the sentimental things he left me, the money he left the boys and the bequests to his personal staff, it all went to you. Nothing has to change right now. He wanted you to decide for yourself what you want to do in the long term. You could go back to school to finish your degree or you could join us at Cruz Saez. He was very firm about me telling you this when the time came. You can decide none of that is for you. If you want to stay home and raise babies or train as a ballerina, your father wanted you to make whatever the best choice is for you with the knowledge that he would have supported it one hundred percent."

I let out a shaky laugh. "He knows I can't dance…"

My words trailed off as I realized I'd just referred to him in the present tense. It was going to be hard to learn not to do that.

"Let me think about all of this," I sighed. "I don't even know where we'd go," I said, gesturing to Mateo.

On the way to the family-only funeral luncheon, Mateo and I talked it over. I had to admit that my father had a point. If I stayed in the villa, I would see him in every corner, every chair, and every room. Mourning was going to be painful wherever I was, but maybe by not doing it in the villa, it could once again become my sanctuary once a bit of time had passed.

"We could go to New York for a few weeks," Mateo offered.

I didn't give a firm answer and forgot about it entirely at the luncheon. Only when we pulled through the gate at the villa did I realize that my father had known me better than I knew myself.

"Yes," I said definitively. "We need to go to New York."

Two days later we were on our way to the city.

I'd expected to sit around in misery, but the morning after we got there, Mateo had suggested—firmly—that I redecorate the apartment for us. I'd resisted at first, but the more he talked about it, the more excited I got. I threw myself into the project, hiring a design assistant to help me choose the materials.

When we went back to Barcelona six weeks later, I had been reset. Not totally—my heart still hurt and I missed my father desperately—but I was better able to focus on the good memories instead of the loss. Mateo and I had set a new wedding date that was several months away. I'd pushed for things to be scaled way back so that it would be family only at the church for the ceremony. I could handle a big reception, but walking down the aisle without my father in front of six hundred people wasn't something I wanted to do. I knew my emotions would be all over the place, so it was smarter to plan around it instead of steering right into it.

A few days after arriving back home, we went to Antonio and Camila's for dinner. We were just finishing the first course when Rafe walked into the room, clearly on edge.

Without any preamble, he blurted, "We need to talk."

I looked at Mateo to see if he had any idea what was up. He shook his head once, letting me know he was clueless.

"I want to start by reminding you all that four years have passed," Rafe said, "so I'm really hoping you can all understand that people change."

My brow had furrowed in confusion before he continued.

"I've been seeing Francesca again..."

I had no real reaction to it, other than the wrinkling of my nose in distaste. How Rafe had been sucked back into her vortex, I didn't know. But the bottom line was that his business was not mine.

"... and now she's pregnant. We're going to have a baby."

Now *that* got my attention. Camila clutched her throat and let out a gasp. Antonio said nothing at first, his shock evident as his mouth opened and closed without any words coming out.

"You're only twenty-one," Camila said, like somehow his youth would have prevented a pregnancy.

"It wasn't planned," Rafe admitted.

Beneath the table, Mateo clutched my hand. I looked over at him, not surprised to find that he looked sad for his brother.

Antonio broke his silence with a harsh sound. "You should have gone away for college," he said.

"I wanted to stay here," Rafe reminded him.

Like me, Rafe had chosen to go to the University of Barcelona. Thankfully I'd never seen Francesca there, but obviously he'd run into her at some point, hence the pregnancy.

"How long have you been seeing her?" Camila asked.

Rafe hung his head and looked away. "Almost six months," he answered.

Antonio cleared his throat and leaned forward, his shoulders rigid with tension. "For six months you have seen this girl and purposely hidden it from us?"

"I knew you'd be mad."

"Mad? *Mad?* I'm not mad, Rafael. I am disappointed in your judgment. What did Francesca have to say about your hiding her?"

"It was kind of her idea. She thought if we introduced it gradually..."

Antonio hadn't been mad before, but that announcement had him clenching his jaw.

"She encouraged you to lie to your family?" Camila asked in a deceptively soft tone.

Rafe shrugged. "No... no! You're twisting it. She just thought it would be easier..."

"If she could get her hooks into you without our interference," Antonio said stiffly.

"You don't even *know* her," Rafe countered.

"I know more than you think," Antonio said. "You have no idea who she is or what you are dealing with, but I do."

"You met her *once* when she was drunk. She's changed."

"You might want to ask your girlfriend how many times she's met me, son. Maybe then you will catch a clue that she is not the misunderstood treasure you think she is."

My brows shot up in surprise. I had no idea what Antonio was talking about.

"What does that mean?"

"It means ask her. Let's see what she says. In the meantime, the question is, what do you intend to do about this, Rafael?"

I bit my lip nervously at the use of Rafe's full name. That was serious.

"I'm going to marry her," he answered.

Mateo stiffened up at the same time I did. As a gotcha baby myself, I had certain feelings about women who trapped men. My last experience with Francesca had been abysmal, so it wasn't like I could grade her on a curve. I couldn't help assuming she was setting a trap. Her family had a business, but they were not wealthy. She had always been envious of Rafe's money, but somehow he hadn't noticed. The way the Cruz brothers had been raised mirrored my own upbringing. Yes, we were ridiculously wealthy, but we had been brought up knowing that didn't mean anything. Not really. We didn't see money as a tool of power—but people like Francesca did.

"And?" Antonio prompted.

"And take care of her and my child," Rafe said, lifting his chin as he stared his father down.

"How?"

"I'll finish school and start working at CS as soon as I do."

"So until then, your mother and I would actually be the ones taking care of things."

Rafe's eyes went wide. "It's not like you don't have it!" he bellowed.

Antonio nodded stiffly. "Yes, son. *We* have it. You do not. You are sorely mistaken if you believe your mother and I will pay for a wedding, pay for your schooling and support *that girl* as she gets her hooks into you for whatever she can get. If you want to marry her, do so knowing that unless Francesca signs an ironclad prenuptial agreement that stipulates she will walk away with not one cent of this family's money *when* you divorce, I will remove you from my will and never acknowledge her or the child."

Camila was openly sobbing by then, and it broke my heart. Standing from my chair, I went and sat next to her, taking her hand in mine in an attempt to provide comfort.

Rafe looked at her in disbelief. "Mom? Are you going to let him do this?"

"That girl is the devil," she choked out through her tears. "You don't know who you are dealing with."

"This is unbelievable! I'm having a goddamn child, and you two are going to pretend it doesn't exist because you don't like the mother? I never would have thought you were this judgmental!"

216

"Rafe—"

"No. You know what? Fuck this. I tried to come here and do the right thing—the way I was raised to do—and you're giving me shit like I'm in the wrong!"

"You were raised not to lie to your family," Antonio snapped, "and yet with Francesca's encouragement that is exactly what you've done for six months!"

"That is such bullshit, Dad—"

Mateo jumped up, having heard enough. Clapping Rafe on the shoulder, he cut him off.

"That is enough," he said in a steely voice. "It is time for you both to go to your corners and make peace with this in your own ways. Nothing good will come from continuing to fight tonight."

Rafe nodded and allowed Mateo to guide him from the room. The second they cleared the doorway Antonio was up and pulling Camila into his arms, holding her as she sobbed against his chest.

Somehow, and I wasn't exactly sure how it went down, Rafe had talked his parents into allowing Francesca to move into their guesthouse with him three weeks later. Marriage was—supposedly—off the table, but they planned to stay together regardless. I remained dubious about the situation.

I'd seen her twice—very briefly—in the weeks since they'd moved in, and both times she'd been perfectly pleasant. From anyone else that would have been great, but I didn't trust her one little bit. One afternoon I was walking down the driveway toward my villa after visiting with Camila for lunch. When I was about halfway down the drive, Francesca called my name. Turning, I found her running toward me, her hand possessively held against her stomach. I stood stiffly, waiting to see what she wanted all while trying to breathe deeply. If she so much as suggested I was fooling around with Rafe, things weren't going to end well.

"What can I do for you, Francesca?" I asked as she came to a halt in front of me.

She fidgeted nervously as her eyes darted around. "I just… I need to apologize for the way I acted that summer. It wasn't right. I know you won't ever forgive me, but I'm hoping we can all get along for the sake of the baby. I mean, you're going to be an aunt," she said with a little laugh.

Mateo and I had already concluded that it was our job to support Rafe and avoid conflict with Francesca at all costs. Antonio refused to tell us when or where he had seen her after the disastrous night of my father's heart attack, so it wasn't as if we had any additional information about her behavior. All any of us knew for certain was that she was pregnant. Six months from now, the first Cruz grandchild would be born. We were a close-knit family which meant that, like it or not, I had to at least be pleasant to her.

"It's okay," I said as convincingly as I could. "We are all very excited about the future and meeting the baby."

Her eyes misted over as she stared at me with hope filled eyes. "Really? My family is not excited at all, so I've been worried no one will really care when the baby comes. I don't want that for my son or daughter."

I felt a twinge of conscience, as I looked her over. I could fault a lot about her, but maybe she really had grown up. Perhaps being pregnant had her turning a new leaf.

# Nineteen

*Ava—the past*

"MI AMOR."

I leaned out of the closet in the guest room and looked to the door where Mateo was standing.

"Hi!" I said cheerfully. "I'm trying to get everything sorted out so we can have this room and the one next door redecorated first—wait. What's wrong?"

I hadn't noticed right away but on closer inspection, his shoulders were stiff as a board and his jaw was like granite.

He stepped into the room, closing the door behind him as he did before crossing the room to me.

"Your mother is here."

I blinked up at him, completely mute for several seconds.

"I'm sorry, what?" I asked.

"Karen is downstairs. I got a call from security an hour ago alerting me that she was at the gate asking to see you. I came home so that we can handle it together. I brought her inside and told her to stay in the sitting room until I came back. The choice is yours, Avelina. If you want me to tell her to leave, I will do it right now. You do not have to see her."

"Why is she here?"

"She says she wants to reconnect with you."

I made an inelegant noise. "It's been years since I've seen or spoken to her."

Mateo nodded but said nothing, letting me work out what course of action I wanted to take. After a minute or so, I took a deep breath and squared my shoulders.

"Fine," I said with a defeated sigh. "Let me go see what she wants."

As ever, he stayed right at my side, holding my hand tightly as we walked downstairs and made our way into the sitting room.

I lost my breath when I saw my mother for the first time after so many years apart. Her face looked the same—surgery, I assumed—but she wasn't weighed down with a fortune in diamonds and pearls. Her outfit, while designer, was far more casual than what I was used to seeing her in.

She stood as I approached her, her eyes filling with tears.

"Lina," she said, her voice trembling.

I stiffened, hating the sound of that stupid name on her lips.

Mateo expelled an angry sounding noise. "Her name is not Lina. You may call her Avelina or Ava. Anything else, and I will escort you from the house without

221

another word."

I fully expected her to snap back since she would have done so in the past. Instead, she hung her head.

"I'm sorry," she sniffed. "I deserved that. Tell me what you want me to call you, honey. Would you prefer Avelina or Ava?"

In all of the years I'd been alive, I could not recall my mother ever asking me what I wanted when it came to my name—or anything else, for that matter.

"Either is fine," I said.

"Then I will call you Ava."

I nodded, uncertain of how to proceed.

"Why are you here, Mother?"

She looked away before bringing her gaze back to me, her lips trembling as she did. "I'd like a name change, too," she answered.

I cocked my head to the side in confusion. "I'm sorry?"

"I want you to call me Mom. Mother is too formal."

I could feel Mateo getting tenser and tenser at my side, so much so he might as well have been carved in stone.

"You want me to call you *mom*?" I asked incredulously.

She nodded. "I... I've come to make amends. I've been doing a lot of work on myself over the last few years. Stomping out of your graduation the way I did was shameful but once it was done, I didn't know how to fix it. At first it was because I had too much stubborn pride, but later it was that so much time was passing. When I saw the news about your father passing I wanted to come support you right then and there, but I knew my presence would only upset you and right then you were dealing with enough. I waited until now in the hopes you'd be more amenable to me trying to mend fences."

I didn't know what to do. I'd been able to relegate her to the back of my mind for years—out of sight, out of mind—because while she wasn't contacting me, I didn't feel there was any hope. Despite my best attempts to let her go entirely, I did love my mother.

"Um…" I turned to Mateo, unable to finish my sentence. He stared at me for several seconds as his eyes searched mine before he nodded and turned to my mother.

"How long are you planning to be in Spain?" he asked.

"As long as it takes," she answered, her eyes on me as she silently implored me to forgive her.

"I can't… not in one day, Mother—I mean, Mom. We'd need to work on this."

She nodded as two tears slid down her cheeks. "Of course. Whatever you want. Maybe I could come back at a better time for you…"

I couldn't believe she was really trying, but there she was, doing the work. I'd never seen my mother so emotional about anything.

"You could stay for a few days," I blurted, surprising myself. "In the guesthouse. We could spend a little bit of time together."

She reached out and grabbed my free hand as she let out a choked sob. "Yes! Of course. Anything you want. I'll stay or I can go if you'd rather not have me here. I'm on your schedule, sweetie."

"Okay. Yes. All right. You'll stay in the guesthouse.

Where are you staying now?"

She named a hotel in Barcelona's city center.

"How about I have a driver take you to retrieve your things?"

"That would be wo-wo-wonderful," she hiccupped as a few more tears slid down her cheeks.

For the first time in years, I found myself hugging my mother. The entire time I wished that my father were still alive so he could help me work out her motives. Did she really want to have a relationship with me—or did she just want to stop her friends talking about her if she wasn't at my wedding?

I hated that I didn't trust her enough to fully believe in her sudden change.

Two and a half weeks later, my mother was still in the guesthouse. Shockingly, she was doing her very best to make inroads with me. I'd been prepared for her to lose interest quickly, but she'd done the exact opposite. She hung on my every word and went out of her way to show me that she was interested in me. Other than a few comments indicating she had some concern about my marrying Mateo when I was *'so young'* she'd been on her best behavior.

She'd even surprised me by making an attempt to be cordial to Antonio and Camila. They were polite but standoffish which I found perfectly acceptable. They'd both seen and heard her at her worst, so they seemed to be waiting for to return to form. So far, that hadn't happened.

In addition to her new attitude and outlook on life, my mother had forged a friendship with Francesca. When I asked why, she explained that she felt sorry for her because she could remember being pregnant and under suspicion. I refrained from pointing out that the suspicion directed at her when she was pregnant with me had been appropriate.

Mother—I was still having trouble thinking of or calling her Mom—was a fountain of information when Francesca was around giving her advice about pregnancy sleep positions and suggestions about how to avoid gaining "massive amounts of baby weight."

When she wasn't fawning over Francesca's small but ever growing belly, she was doing her best to help me with the wedding. She seemed sad that there wasn't a lot to do since I'd been ready for it before Papá had passed. I didn't want to hurt her by pointing out that Camila had helped me do everything. Instead, I tried to make her feel useful where I could.

"Moth—Mom," I called out as I knocked on the door to the guesthouse.

She came to the door with a smile before hugging me and dropping a kiss on my cheek. "Are we doing anything special today?"

"Camila and I are going into town to assemble bags at the food bank. Would you like to come?"

Her face fell. "Oh, honey, I'd love to, but honestly, I'm not feeling myself right now."

She looked absolutely fine—practically the picture of health. "Is everything okay?"

She nodded. "Yes—it's just a small headache."

"Do you need anything? I could stay..."

"No, honey. You go right on down there and do your work. I know how important it is for you."

I left her with a promise I'd check on her later and then headed out with Camila. We put in a wonderful three hours at the food bank before heading home. I was busy texting dirty things to Mateo as the car wove its way through the streets when Camila let out a loud gasp.

"Stop the car!" she yelled.

My face was on fire as I tossed the phone into my purse, mortified that she must have seen the things Mateo and I were saying to each other. God, I thought, she must think we are the biggest perverts on earth.

"I'm sorry—"

"Ava, look!"

She had turned and was looking out the rearview window, her arm held out and pointing to someone on the sidewalk. I narrowed my eyes and focused, a gasp of my own escaping me when I saw what, and who, she was pointing at.

Just twenty feet from us, Francesca was standing on the sidewalk talking animatedly to someone. What made her being there gasp-worthy was that she was wearing a pair of jeans and a tank top—and the four and a half month bump we'd gotten used to was nowhere to be found. Her stomach was flat as a board, her navel on full display.

Before I could stop her, Camila was climbing out of the car. I slid across the seat after her at the same time security flung the doors open and scurried to us so that they flanked us on either side as we walked toward Francesca.

We were almost on top of her when she finally turned and noticed us. When she did, she lost all the color in her face.

"What—why—what are you doing down here?" she asked.

"Never mind why we are here," Camila snapped. "You lied to my son! You aren't pregnant at all!"

For just a second Francesca dropped all pretenses, the awful and calculating personality I'd known four years before making itself known. Just as quickly she got control of it, her eyes filling with tears—obviously fake—as she wrung her hands in front of her.

"I was!" she cried, her voice sounding hysterical, but forced. "I lost the baby and I didn't know how to tell anyone."

I knew she was lying. It was so obvious a blind person would have seen it. A feeling of rage flew through my veins as I glared at her. Her actions were currently hurting Camila, but they would destroy Rafe, someone who had never done anything but defend her. I wanted to tear her limb from limb.

"When?" I asked.

Her eyes were diamond hard as she glared at me before remembering to school her expression.

"Last week," she answered, frowning down at the ground like the memory was too awful for her to handle.

"What hospital?"

Her mouth opened and closed several times as the gears turned in her head. Francesca was evil, but she wasn't stupid. A hospital meant records.

"I—it happened at my family's restaurant. In the bathroom."

"And what happened after?" I pressed.

"I dealt with it."

"How?"

"I cleaned myself up and took some aspirin."

"So you never went to the hospital or saw a doctor for it?"

"I didn't need to."

"You're a horrible liar," I said as I stepped in closer to her, wanting her to know I was about four seconds away from slapping her silly.

"I'm not lying!"

"Shut your mouth," Camila snapped, walking forward until she was right in Francesca's face. "Let me tell you how I know you didn't lose a baby, Francesca. Maybe you'll learn something about how pregnancy works. At almost five months pregnant, a miscarriage would've been painful. Regardless of how quickly it happened, you would have needed a D&C after it was over. I know because I had it happen to me. That's not something you take aspirin for."

"It wasn't the other day, okay? Are you happy? I lost my baby months ago!"

"Another lie," I seethed. "You are rotten to your core."

"And you're a fucking cunt," she spat.

I smiled because she'd played right into my hands. "I knew your whole goody-goody act was too good to be true."

Camila stepped forward and got right into Francesca's face. When her bodyguard tried to step in, Camila held up a hand and told him to step back. Through it all, she kept her eyes trained on Francesca.

"This is the second time you've cried wolf where pregnancy is concerned to my family. There will not be a third time," Camila said, her voice menacingly cold. "This is the end of the road for you. If I find you talking to or breathing near anyone I love, I will destroy you—and your family. Do not test me, little girl."

I was damn proud of Camila's mama bear attitude. She was the softest and sweetest woman alive, but if you messed with her family, she was clearly ready to throw down. I applauded her for it.

When we got back to the car, it hit me that she'd said it was the second time Francesca had done something with a pregnancy.

"What did you mean about it being the second time she cried wolf?"

Camila sighed and patted my hand. "She showed up in Antonio's office a week after the party four years ago and told him she was pregnant with Rafe's baby. She claimed her family wouldn't support her, so she begged him for money to have an abortion. He did. Almost a year later, she came back with an audio recording of him forcing money on her to get an abortion. She told him she'd take it to Rafe if he didn't pay. Antonio gave her ten thousand dollars and told her if she ever came back with that tape, he'd have her arrested for extortion.

"She wasn't smart enough to notice either of the times she was there, that there are the signs in the lobby and in the elevators advising that by entering Cruz Saez you acknowledge that you can and will be recorded at any time. Ever since the phony sexual harassment messiness that happened between the secretary and our VP all those years ago, Antonio and your father had taken preventive measures. You know the drill. Unless the conversation was happening between Antonio and Joaquin, or it involved the family, everything is recorded. I'm sure it's no surprise to you that the version Francesca blackmailed him with didn't match up to what really happened. I don't really know why he didn't tell Rafael right then and there what she did, but when she never came back, we figured it was over."

My mind was officially blown by the depths Francesca had sunk in order to perpetrate her lies. The girl was a nightmare. When we got home, Camila sent security out to the guesthouse to toss her. They came back half an hour later with a suitcase they found hidden under the bed. In it there were four pregnancy bellies of differing sizes. I left when Antonio got home, his face green as he walked toward Camila. They needed alone time, so I went back to the villa and waited for Mateo to come home. I knew he wouldn't be far behind his father—one look at Antonio indicated something was seriously wrong and Mateo wouldn't have missed that.

When he arrived home and I told him everything, he seethed with anger before his emotions swung the other way.

"Rafe is going to be devastated by this," he said.

I knew he was right. I also knew there was nothing we could do to spare him the pain.

# Twenty

*Ava—present*

I CAME TO IN THE POOL WITH MATEO'S ARMS AROUND me as he raced us toward the steps. He moved fast, climbing out of the water and onto the deck with a speed that stunned me. I sucked in a breath and then another, trying to get myself calmed down. Mateo didn't notice because he was frantically running into the living room while he had a loud conversation with God about giving me a break.

When I patted his shoulder and said his name to get his attention, he stopped dead in his tracks and looked down at me with obvious anxiety.

"I am calling for an ambulance," he assured me.

I shook my head. "No. I'm fine."

"You are not fine," he retorted. "You had some kind of episode and then fainted dead away."

"I had a panic attack and hyperventilated my way into passing out," I admitted. "It isn't a medical thing, baby. It was all mental."

He started walking again, taking me directly into our bedroom. Setting me down on the bed, he cupped my face, as he looked me over.

"Be straight with me, Ava. Are you certain it was a panic attack?"

I looked him straight in the eye so he would know I was serious. "I am absolutely positive. I remembered, Mateo. Everything."

His expression changed to one of understanding as he nodded. "Wait here. I will get our robes."

"No! Don't leave me," I cried. "Take me with you."

He lifted me up and hugged me to him as he walked us through the bathroom and into the closet. "I have you and I will never let you go."

I stayed as close to him as possible when he set me down and grabbed my robe. Pulling it around me from the back, he helped me put my arms inside and then pulled it together in the front before belting it.

Taking my hand in his, he guided me to his side of the closet where he pulled his own on. As soon as he had it belted, he took my hand again and walked with me into the bedroom. When we got there he sat on the bed and then pulled me into his lap so he could hold onto me while we talked.

"What made you remember?"

I took a deep breath and answered, "When you mentioned the night we made love in the pool. It happened the night before the accident. We were being so quiet because my mother was on the other side of the fence in the guesthouse.

"When I—" I paused, swallowing thickly before I

could continue. "I remember now that when I heard the tape, my very first reaction was to laugh. The whole thing was preposterous. I knew you loved me and I only had to refer to the night before in my memory for a solid example of you, when we were in the pool, telling me over and over again that you worshiped me and would spend your life making sure I remembered that every minute of every day. I knew a man who didn't want to marry his fiancée wouldn't be next to, under, on top of or inside of that woman at every available opportunity."

"I am relieved to hear that you did not immediately believe that garbage," he murmured. "It killed me that the only thing you could remember from the day was listening to the tape. You were so angry, so adamant that what you had heard was true."

My lower lip quivered as I nodded. "I'm so sorry," I sniffed. "I don't think I could handle the truth."

"Tell me everything you remember," he instructed.

So I did.

# Twenty-One

*Ava—the day of the accident*

I WAS GLAD I HADN'T MOVED THE WEDDING DATE forward as much as Mateo had wanted me to. Rafe had been a mess and I knew a wedding would only upset him more. He was angry at Francesca—very much so—but he was also mourning the loss of the pregnancy he'd believed was real.

In addition to the anxiety we were all feeling for Rafe, I was having some issues with my mother. Her sweet disposition was walking itself back a little bit more each day and she'd gone from making small comments about my marrying Mateo to straight out saying—frequently—that I was too young to get married.

I'd had enough of her constantly being around. Having a relationship with her was one thing, but seeing her every day was too much. To that end, I sat her down to discuss her return to New York..

I could tell she was miffed by the suddenness, but honestly, I didn't care. She needed to go. Having her around was stressing me out and when I was like that it left Mateo on permanent high alert. With what was happening with Rafe there was more than enough going on in our family. I didn't need my mother adding to the stress. Simply put, she had to go.

The Cruz Saez jet was scheduled to take her back to New York just before six at night, so we were meeting for a late lunch in town. She'd made some noises about shopping before she left, something I had no interest in. Mateo and Antonio had been more keyed up than I'd ever seen them for the last three days and I knew it was one hundred percent because of Rafe. I understood there was nothing I could do to ease the burden for them, but worrying about Mateo in particular meant I wasn't interested in shopping.

In the end, I gave my mother the keys to the Audi my father had bought me for my twentieth birthday and sent her on her way with my black Amex. She'd put up some token resistance to taking it, but the way her eyes lit up when she saw the card was a clear indicator that she wanted it.

"I don't need your money. I can afford to shop," she assured me.

Since I was choosing not to spend her final day in Spain with her shopping, I felt like I owed it to her.

"It's no problem, Moth—erm, Mom. Take it and have a good time. I'll meet you at the restaurant at three."

"I—this isn't something I need," she insisted. "I don't want you thinking I came here for this."

I patted her hand gently. "It will make me happy to know that you're having fun. Don't give it another thought—it's just money."

"If you're sure…"

"I'm positive. Go shop until you *almost* drop. Just leave yourself enough energy for lunch."

She practically skipped out to the car. Seeing how excited she was assuaged my guilt for forcing her back to New York before she'd asked to go and for ditching out on her for the majority of her final day. I'd inherited an embarrassing amount of money that I couldn't possibly hope to spend in five lifetimes. As far as I was concerned, she could enjoy the day on me.

Security drove me into town where I met up with my mother at the quiet restaurant we'd agreed upon earlier. Since she'd driven my Audi into town I instructed them to wait for us in the parking lot so that they could take her to the airport after lunch, while I would drive my car home with the second team tailing. Honestly, it was why I chose not to drive a lot of the time. If security was going to be there anyway, it made more sense just to get into the Suburban and leave the driving to them. Mateo enthusiastically encouraged me to continue on like that.

My mother and I sat in a side room I'd reserved a few days before. I'd expected her to be on a shopping high, but instead she was incredibly fidgety. It was obvious she was worried about something and the way her eyes kept darting around the room was making me edgy. After the waitress dropped off the entrees we'd ordered I addressed the elephant in the room.

"All right, what's going on with you?" I asked.

Mother fiddled with the stem of her wineglass before looking up at me with eyes full of tears. Something about it felt wrong. Forced, like bad performance art.

"I was approached by a stranger while I was shopping," she said.

It hung out there over us for several seconds while I waited for her to enlighten me. When she didn't, I moved my hand in a circle to indicate she should get on with it.

"Got it. Approached while shopping. Then what?"

"Well," she began, wringing her hands nervously before she moved on to twisting her cloth napkin.

"Mother, focus."

"I was given an iPod and a flash drive."

My eyebrows went up in confusion. "So you won something, then? Like a gift?"

She shook her head and sniffled before bringing the napkin up and dabbing at her dry looking eyes. Every single thing she was a show, her affectations deliberate.

"Not a gift," she answered. "A nightmare."

She leaned over and pulled something a small silver iPod out of her purse. I recognized the red bag as being a Louis Vuitton Lockit—I had the same one in a different color—and since she hadn't had it before, I knew she'd spent some time at the Louis store earlier in the day. When I looked at her hand as she slid the iPod across the table to me, I noticed she'd also acquired a rose gold Rolex with diamonds on the faceplate and all around the band, along with several pearl and diamond bracelets. It was like stepping back in time to the mother I'd grown up with, and I wondered how much she'd spent.

I glanced down at the iPod she put in front of me and

then raised an eyebrow. "I don't need one," I said dryly.

"No," she said as she leaned forward. "Listen to it."

I barely refrained from rolling my eyes as I slid the ear buds into my ears and touched the device so it would start. As there was only one track on it, I easily deduced what she wanted me to listen to.

Mateo's voice filled my ears. As I listened to the conversation, I quickly realized my mother had absolutely not been approached by a stranger. Francesca had given her the iPod. I knew this because hers was the second voice on the recording.

*"How cute that you believe you can come here and give orders. We are in charge, not you."*

*"Really, Mateo? Because from where I'm sitting, it looks like I've got the goods. How do you think the little heiress would feel if I told her you were only marrying her because your father is forcing you to?"*

My blood ran cold through my veins and my eyes felt like two diamonds as I half-listened to the recording and stared at my mother across the table. I'd been such an idiot to have thought for even one second that she had changed.

*"You can say whatever you want," Mateo chided. "It will not matter. She does… as I say."*

*"I bet you won't be if I show her all of my evidence against you. Your father can't afford to buy her out. The only way to retain absolute control is to marry her and get her half of the company signed over to you."*

*"So what? You think I am not prepared for that? I handle things. It is what I do."*

*"Maybe," Francesca drawled. "But I think if she knew*

*you've been cheating on her for years, she might get a little angry. You've played her for a fool."*

"Who and when I fuck is none of your business," he snapped. "Avelina… is too damn stupid to stop me. I have come this far without her knowing a thing. Do you really think I would let you ruin that now?"

"What I know is that if you don't pay me, she'll know everything."

"She would not believe you."

"I am betting it will give her pause."

Silence, and then, "You are quite something," he laughed. "Tell me what you want."

"Twenty-five million dollars wired directly into an off-shore account."

"You have the number?" he asked.

"Yes."

"It will be done immediately."

I pulled the earphones out when the recording stopped. The whole thing was pathetic. A poorly hacked conversation that had been manipulated to within an inch of its life. I would have known regardless of the fact that I knew she'd blackmailed Antonio with a fake recording before, but it didn't hurt that I was one hundred percent sure.

After I wrapped the earphones around the iPod, I dropped it into my purse. I rolled my shoulders as I looked across the table at my mother, cataloging her features because I'd decided it was over, for good. This would be the last time I saw her.

"Please give me my car keys and my credit card," I instructed.

"I—sure, of course."

I went to stand once she'd pushed them across the table to me, but she stopped me.

"*Where are you going*?" she asked frantically.

I sat back down, crossing my arms over my chest as I stared at her.

"I'm going home. Your attempt to manipulate me was an extraordinary failure."

"Me- me?" she spluttered. "You think I had anything to do with that?"

"Yes. I know it came from Francesca and I know you were close to her. What's your end game here, really? Do you imagine maybe I won't marry Mateo? Then what? I move back to New York to support you to the manner in which you became accustomed when my father was alive?"

Her face paled as she shook her head. "No! I—yes, it was Francesca who gave me the iPod. But she did so because she's blackmailing me, Lina."

"This ought to be rich," I mocked. "What is she blackmailing you for, Mother?"

Tears streaked down her cheeks as she looked at me beseechingly.

"I never wanted you to know this, but I have no choice. I'm so sorry."

"You're quickly coming to the end of my patience. Spit it out," I snapped.

"Joaquin… wasn't your biological father. I was sleeping with another man."

For a few seconds, it felt like the world had stopped turning. I shook my head in denial and slashed my hand through the air in anger. What she had just done was lower than low—absolutely unforgivable.

"*Lies!*" I seethed. "How dare you say that to me when he is no longer alive to counter your ridiculous claims."

I stood up fast, knocking the chair I'd been sitting over because I'd pushed it back too hard. My mother jumped up too, grabbing my forearms to hold me in place.

"It's true," she cried. "I never wanted you to know—I would not have told you—but the evidence is on the flash drive. Your father knew. It's how I got you back when you were five. Everyone has known but you. Mateo has been aware for years and he never said a word to you."

"It's not true. I am my father's child."

"In personality, maybe. Genetically, you were never his daughter. Think about it. It's why no one ever believes you're Spanish, Lina. Your real father was an American valet attendant at the club I worked for."

My anger was like a living, breathing entity. If she were telling the truth, I would never, ever forgive her. Losing my father had rocked me to my foundation—for her to add on to that pain was the lowest form of human cruelty. No loving mother would ever hurt their child the way she was hurting me. I shook her off and pulled away from her clutches.

"I'm leaving," I said, my voice hard even to my own ears.

"Would you prefer to have lived the remainder of your life with your head in the sand?"

"I can't believe you're doing this. How could you?"

My hands were shaking as I grabbed the keys off the table, before noticing the flash drive was still sitting there.

I plucked that up, surprised when she tried to grab it from me.

"That isn't yours!" she hissed.

We had a tug of war over it that I easily won. I glared at her as I tossed it into my purse.

Without another word I spun on my heel and headed directly out the door. I left security behind to deal with getting my mother to the airport and got into my car to go to Mateo. If anything my mother had said were true, he would tell me. And if he didn't know, we would find out together. My hands shook and my stomach churned sickly as I clutched the wheel. I could handle whatever the answer was, I promised myself. No matter what I found out, my father would always be my father. Nothing could take that away.

I wished assuring myself of that would make my tears dry up, but it wasn't working. The more I thought that it might be true, the sicker I felt. Had my father kept it from me my whole life?

Those questions took a backseat when I realized someone was right on my bumper, driving very aggressively. I shrieked as the car hit my bumper. Stepping on the gas, I tried to outdrive whoever the idiot was behind me. Their rate of speed picked up as mine did, and anytime they had the chance, they would smash into me again. As I rounded the next turn, the car slammed into me from behind, sending the Audi forward in such a way that I couldn't control it. I screamed as the car slammed into something, the sound of shattering glass and twisting steel the last things I heard before I passed out.

# Twenty-Two

*Mateo—present*

F OR MONTHS I HAD BEEN CONVINCED THE psychological trauma Ava had suffered that day stemmed from her mother trying to extort her for money. There had never been any evidence to contradict that. While the iPod in her purse had contained the butchered conversation I had had when Francesca tried—and failed—to weasel money from my family, the flash drive Ava had in her purse had been blank.

Every doctor and therapist I consulted with had told me in no uncertain terms that the confrontation with her mother followed by the accident—both things happening on the heels of losing her father—had caused her to shut down. It turned out we had all been wrong. It was not the trauma of her mother turning on her at all.

What she had been so desperate not to remember revolved around Karen telling her Joaquin had not been her biological father. I did not believe that craziness for a second. Ava was nothing like Karen because she was her father's daughter through and through. So much so, I would have been more inclined to believe Karen was not her mother before I ever thought Joaquin was not biologically tied to her. I held her close as she finished her story.

"Do you know if anything she said was true?" Ava asked.

I shook my head emphatically. "Of course not. If I knew something like that, I would have told you. You and I have no secrets, ever. I do not think you have anything to worry about, mi amor. I would bet Karen was not telling you the truth."

"Your father will know," she murmured. "My father would have told him. I know it. We need to call him."

I glanced at the bedside table and noted it was just before ten at night in Spain. Hoping my father was still awake I lifted the cordless from its base and placed the call. He answered on the second ring.

"What's up?" he asked.

"Avelina has remembered what happened the day of her accident. We need to talk to you about what her memories entailed."

"Of course. Anything I can do to help, I'm here. Is she okay?"

"Shaken but holding up okay at the moment," I said. "I am going to put you on speaker while I explain everything she remembers."

When I got to the part about Joaquin not being Ava's biological parent, my father let out a thunderous sound.

"I will destroy that goddamn lying bitch if it is the last thing I do," he growled.

"Does that mean it's not true?" Ava asked, her voice

trembling with emotion.

"*No*, sweetheart. It is one hundred percent not true," my father stated categorically. "Joaquin was your father in every way."

"You're sure?" she asked, her voice hesitant. "What if what she told me was true, but Papá never knew?"

My father sighed, a sound of anxiety I could almost feel.

"I hate her for putting you in this position, Avelina. This is not something you should ever have had to know. I hope you do not think less of me for what I am about to tell you."

Ava's eyes were wide as she waited for my father to say whatever it was that was making him sound anxious.

"I never liked or trusted Karen. When you were born, I begged Joaquin to have a DNA test run to be certain you were his. I want you to know that he would have kept you regardless. It was me who pushed for it, me who insisted he needed to know if Karen was manipulating him more than we already thought. The DNA only confirmed what your father knew all along—you were his ángel."

She sagged against me in relief, sniffling as tears began sliding down her cheeks.

"I'm not upset, Tío. I am thankful that decision you made all those years ago was able to put my mind at ease now."

"Put this behind you now," he said. "She has done enough damage. If your father were here, this would have killed him. Her cruelty knows no bounds. If you are willing, I would like to move on your behalf to have her evicted from the apartment Joaquin let her live in for all of these years. This would have been the final straw for him, Ava. He would want you to sever all ties."

Her brows shot up in confusion. "Have I been paying for that?" she asked.

"Well, no. As you know, their deal was that until you graduated college he would continue to pay. At the time of his death he was still paying for the apartment and giving her the hundred thousand a month in child support. I didn't want to upset you so I took over. I was going to talk to you about it but life kept getting in the way."

"Cut her off," she said firmly. "She is gone to me. I will never speak to her again."

"You see? You really are your father's daughter," my father said proudly. "I will take care of it. I hope having all of the answers to your questions helps, sweetheart. With Karen out of the picture and Francesca in jail, everything has been resolved."

Ava sat up fast. "You didn't tell me you had her arrested for her fake tapes and money grabs," she whispered to me.

I raised my hand as a sign to give me a moment.

"Thank you for clearing this up, Pop. I will call you tomorrow."

After I set the phone on the side table, I turned back to my woman and ran my fingers through her hair. There was one more piece to the puzzle that she did not know and it was time for me to tell her.

"Francesca is not just in jail because she manipulated recordings and asked for money."

Her brows rose in confusion. "This ought to be rich," she huffed. "What else did she do?"

I swallowed past the anger that clawed from inside my throat whenever I thought of Francesca.

"She ran you off the road and straight into a pole," I answered. "On purpose."

The color leeched from Ava's face as she gaped at me. *"What?"*

"She confessed to the whole thing," I explained. "They—she and Karen—wanted to break us up. Karen was doing it for money; Francesca did it for spite. Since she never once mentioned the whole not your father thing, I have to assume she did not know. What she *did* know was when and where you were meeting your mother for lunch. She claims it was not pre-meditated. She was circling the restaurant in the hopes of seeing you upset. When you emerged and got into the car, she followed you. She is trying to say she temporarily went insane. I do not think it will fly at sentencing. The bitch is as guilty as a person can be."

"She's insane, but there's nothing temporary about it," Ava replied coldly. "I can't believe she almost killed me. Half a foot more to the left and I would've been dead on the spot."

My chest constricted in agony. "I know," I murmured. "Seeing the wreckage afterward, waiting nineteen hours for you to wake up… it was hell."

"And now that nightmare is over," she said. "Never again will we be apart. I'm so sorry—"

I covered her lips with my finger. "What did I tell you about apologizing for what you did not do?"

"It *was* me though," she answered through trembling lips. "I am the one who forced you to let me go. I am the one who told you I didn't want to marry you. How can you forgive me for that?"

I hugged her to me tightly. "There is nothing to forgive. I love you. I have always loved you and I will always love you. Do not dwell on what can not be changed, mi amor."

She wrapped her arms around me and held me like I was a human anchor.

"I love you," she whispered. "Thank you for never, ever giving up."

"Giving up is never an option where you are concerned," I said, my voice thick with emotion.

We stayed that way for several minutes, holding each other and kissing softly. When she was fully settled again, I slid her off my lap and sat her on the edge of the bed. I got off the mattress and kneeled before her.

"I am hoping this all means that you will say yes to the question I am about to ask."

My heart started beating again normally when she nodded her head. For the first time in months, things were exactly the way they were meant to be.

"Will you marry me?" I asked.

She dropped off of the bed and wrapped her arms around me as she cried.

"Always yes, Mateo. Always."

I took her face in my hands and stared down at her with a grin.

"Then you know what you need to do, mi amor. Get your ring so I can put it back where it belongs."

She stood and quickly ran into the closet. I followed behind her, laughing to myself as she opened one of her drawers and pulled the velvet box from a pair of jeans. Only Ava would put a priceless ring in a pair of old jeans. After she closed the drawer she turned and handed me the box. Something inside of me settled when I opened it and saw it again for the first time in months. Pulling it out, I held it out as she raised her hand.

"This makes it official," I said. "In five weeks time, you will meet me at the end of the aisle."

She sniffled as I slid it back onto her finger where it belonged. "If you'd like, I will run to you," she said softly.

My heart felt like it might burst from joy. "Or you could torture me a little and walk slow," I joked. "You are always worth the wait."

# *Epilogue*

"YOU MAY KISS THE BRIDE."

I gasped as my husband pulled me in close and kissed me—deeply and without any regard for our applauding family.

We only broke apart when the priest cleared his throat. Keeping me close, Mateo swiped his thumb below my lower lip.

"Te amo, Señora Cruz."

"Te amo, Señor Cruz."

Linking our fingers, he turned us to face our family. I'd gotten the small wedding I needed—only Mateo's father, his brothers and Camila in attendance—and we would be spending the rest of the evening celebrating with the six hundred people we'd invited to the reception.

As we stepped down from the altar to the aisle, I turned and looked back at my father's urn with a smile. Antonio had carried it down the aisle ahead of me before setting it down in a place of importance. Physically, my father had not made it to the wedding, but I swore I'd been able to feel him around me all day. I had no doubt he was up in heaven celebrating my marriage right along with us.

"Mi hermosa esposa," Mateo called out as he came into the villa.

I grinned as I stood from the desk in my home office and raced down the stairs into my husband's waiting arms.

"I'm very proud of you for lasting a whole seven hours at work today," I teased as he swung me around.

"Only because there was a meeting," he admitted.

In the year and a half that had passed since he brought me back after our nine-week separation, he'd consistently only gone in for short amounts of times, choosing to work from home so he could be as close to me as possible. Our month long honeymoon in Bora Bora had been like heaven. When we came back, I'd been certain he would settle back into his previous eight to ten hour a day schedule, but that hadn't happened. In fact, for our first wedding anniversary three months prior, he'd insisted on taking me to Tahiti for four weeks.

I wasn't complaining at all. No amount of time together ever felt like too much, or even enough. We were selfish for each other, always wanting more. I knew the way we loved each other was a gift and I gave thanks for it, and him, every single day.

Without warning, he lifted me up into his arms and strode up the stairs to our bedroom.

"Seven hours was too much. I missed you terribly."

"I can tell," I said cheekily as he set me down on the bed.

"I came within five seconds of telling everyone to shut up so I could come home. You know what that means, right?"

"That you're a stubborn, bossy alpha who needed to get back to his woman?" I cracked.

"Well, that too," he laughed as he pulled off my sandals and began massaging my right foot. "Mostly it means I am addicted to you."

"It must be tough," I sighed blissfully as he rubbed the arch of my foot just so.

He tickled the bottom of my foot and laughed when I let out a little screech.

"Not so tough that I would ever change it," he answered as he went back to rubbing the sole of my foot.

"I'm addicted to you, too. I'm good with there being no cure."

Letting go of my foot, he came down over me on the bed, dropping soft kisses all across my neck and chin before claiming my mouth and kissing me deeply.

"It seems you missed me just as much," he rasped when he pulled back.

I bit my lip and nodded. He had no idea.

"I need to get you naked," he announced.

The way he said it, I knew he did not want my help. I moved only to make his job easier as he peeled off my top, shorts, bra and underwear. When he had me naked, I enjoyed the show as he divested himself of his business attire. I whistled as he took his shirt off and dropped it on the floor.

"You make this whole suit thing look good," I said happily. "Your wife is one lucky woman."

"I am the lucky one," he rasped. "So perfect, even the sound of your voice makes me hard," he said as he pulled his belt from his pants.

I didn't immediately respond because he had undone his pants and was pulling them down along with his boxer briefs.

"So I should keep talking?" I asked a little breathlessly.

"Sí," he growled.

As usual I forgot how to speak in full and coherent sentences when he came down on top of me and began making his way down my body. He paid particular attention to my breasts, sucking and licking each nipple over and over again as I gripped his forearms and writhed beneath him.

When he had me almost out of my mind with desire, he dropped from my breasts to my stomach. His tongue danced across my flesh before he dipped and swirled in and around my bellybutton a half dozen times before continuing lower.

"Legs over my shoulders."

I followed instruction as he moved down to where I needed him the most. I shivered as I complied, leaving myself open for him.

"It appears you were missing me almost as much as I missed you," he said huskily.

"More," I answered.

He smiled up at me from between my legs as he leaned in close and traced his tongue up and down between my delicate folds. The heat of his mouth and tongue on me always made me crave him even more. I slid my fingers into his hair and moaned as he licked and sucked every single part of me. When he spread me wider and speared his tongue into me, my hands went right to my breasts as I arched my back and pinched my nipples. He slid his tongue out and returned it to my clit before sucking it in and working the top with the tip of his tongue.

"Mateo," I cried as he kept going, bringing me right to the edge.

Two fingers slid inside, rubbing against the front of me as he continued to work his tongue on my clit.

"Yes, yes, I'm about to—yes!"

He didn't stop until every last bit of ecstasy had been wrung from my body. I was a breathless mess as he came up over me, fisting his length as he rubbed the tip through my arousal.

"Now," he growled as he pushed in deep, filling me in one hard thrust.

"It is always *so* good," he groaned into my mouth as he began pushing in and out.

I loved the way his chest rubbed up against mine as he began going harder, our bodies slick with sweat from the exertion. His hands were braced on either side of my head, while mine were holding on tight to his arms as he thrust.

"God, Mateo," I cried as he began thrusting faster.

"Yes, baby, that's it," I yelled, squeezing around him as he began thrusting faster.

He sat up so he could grab my knees, pushing them back toward my chest as he slammed into me harder.

"Harder," I cried. "Yes!"

"Touch your clit, mi amor."

I let out a needy cry as I ran my finger over my clit before beginning to make small circles.

"I… oh, yeah, oh, Mateo, yes! I'm coming," I yelled as I seized up around him, my pleasure growing exponentially when he yelled my name as he started filling me with his hot release. We shivered and shook together until we were both finished.

He rolled us onto our sides and pulled me against his chest protectively as he ran his fingers through my scalp.

"And *that* is how you spend an afternoon," he said breathlessly. "Forget that whole work thing. It is never as important as you are."

I chuckled as I snuggled in close to my husband, the man who made every day an adventure. I loved him to the point of distraction, literally, and I knew I always would. There was nothing better than that.

The End

The Enamorado series will continue with Alejandro's book, "I Want".
Releasing Summer 2017.
Join the Enamorado Facebook group for sneak peeks and teasers.
www.facebook.com/groups/1923765301243538

Visit my I Don't Pinterest board to see some of my visual inspirations!
www.pinterest.com/AuthorEllaFox/i-dont

I Don't Playlist

*Escape*–Enrique Iglesias

*I Won't Give Up*–Jason Mraz

*Yellow*–Coldplay

*Somewhere Only We Know*–Keane

*Hit The Ground Runnin'*–Keith Urban

*Won't Go Home Without You*–Maroon 5

*Stay With You*–The Goo Goo Dolls

Check out the playlist on Spotify
open.spotify.com/user/12129123335/playlist/6OHOIiHg-
1ZY4FkP2S39cWU

# Acknowledgements

As I sit down to write these I am reminded once again of the fact that no book is ever finished without help. Thank you to everyone who got me across the finish line.

First, MASSIVE thanks to Yahaira Martinez for taking the time to help me with my Spanish. You were a lifesaver!

Thank you to Sommer Stein for nailing this cover. It is, hands down, my favorite cover ever. I say that every time and somehow, some way, you continue to knock it out of the park and make each and every one even better!

Major thanks and appreciation go out to Ellie McLove for the edit, Judy Zweifel for the proofing, and Stacey Blake for making my baby pretty.

Thanks to my mom and my nephew for putting up with my vampire business hours! It's how I roll and you don't question it.

Thanks again to Rochelle who read every word of this story probably a dozen times as I worked and then re-worked things along the way. I more than appreciate that you loved Mateo and Avelina as much as I do.

Thank you to all of my friends who no longer question why I hermit away in the writing cave for weeks on end—even when I've been wearing the same pair of pajamas for days and my hair looks like an eagles nest.

And, finally, thank you to all of the authors, bloggers and readers who make this job such a joy.

# About the Author

Ella Fox is the *USA Today* Bestselling Author of Consequences of Deception, The Hart Family series & many other sexy and exciting books.

Ella loves music, photography and comedy movies. She's an all around goofball. She grew up loving to read, especially romance. That's not surprising considering the fact that her mom is *USA Today* Bestselling Author Suzanne Halliday.

www.pinterest.com/AuthorEllaFox

Like Ella on Facebook
www.facebook.com/EllaFoxAuthor

Follow Ella on Twitter www.twitter.com/AuthorEllaFox

# Other Books